Thank you [illegible]

Support!

Stephanie Nicole Norris

MW00942772

# Mistaken Identity

by

STEPHANIE NICOLE NORRIS

Copyright © 2016 by Stephanie Nicole Norris

All rights reserved. No part of this book may be reproduced or transmitted in any form or by any means without written permission of the author except in the case brief quotations embodied in critical articles or reviews.

This is a work of fiction. The events and characters described here are imaginary and are not intended to refer to specific places or persons dead or alive. Any resemblances are purely coincidental.

# Acknowledgments

It gives me great pleasure to be able to write and publish my sixth novel. It is a blessing that I am truly happy to receive. Thank you goes out to my Lord and Savior, Jesus Christ, who I am nothing without. Thank you to my Mom; Jessica Ward who I love always and forever. Thanks for being a blessing in my life and always having my back. You mean the world to me, words cannot describe how I feel about you. I would like to thank my sisters for having my back whenever I need them. You ladies are a strong set of women and I love and appreciate everything that you do April Moseley and Aliesha Ward.

I would like to thank all of my family and friends who have been with me throughout my journey of life. Thank you to the authors that have become a part of my life and/or been helpful and welcomed me as a new author into this literary world. I appreciate the warm welcome, fellow comrades. I salute you.

Shout out to my readers!!!!

I would also like to thank Junnita Jackson who put together this stunning book cover. My editor, Tina Nance of Perfect Prose Editing, once again you did a wonderful job. Thank you.

To my beautiful blessing, Noah Brewer, I have been blessed to have you a part of my life. I love you more than words can say my son. If I left any names out don't hold it against me, I thank you too!

# Prologue

"Tiana you're being unreasonable! We look identical. How could you be this vain? You could have any man you want, and you have the nerve to tell me my husband belongs to you! Are you crazy?"

Briana, made a left turn on the ramp and merged onto 285 NE. Traffic was light for the moment, but it never stayed that way on Atlanta highways. Heat sizzled from Briana's ears like a chimney, making her turn on the air. Her twin sister, Tiana, had threatened Briana in the worst way, and she was so mad her body felt on fire.

"Oh shut up!" Tiana yelled. "Identical or not, I have been holding this in for a long time. Why do I have to have someone who looks exactly like me? I don't feel like my own person! I feel like someone has taken over my life! I don't want a twin. I don't want to share my parents! When it comes to my career, my love life, my finances, I'm done competing with you! And that man you call a husband approached me first, he wanted to take me out. He had no way of knowing I had a twin sister who loved to have everything I have, even my looks!"

"I can't help it because we're twins! I didn't ask to look like you! Listen, you really sound insane right now. I don't even know where all this is coming from," Briana said.

"Just admit it, Briana, you've always wished you were me. Your friends act stuck up and they're forever turning their nose up at me. And you act like they're just as sweet as pie. You're a phony just like they are!"

"But I never treated you that way, so why take this out on me? Why haven't you ever sat down with me and had a conversation about this?"

"Oh, please, like you didn't know! It doesn't even matter. I won't sit in the background and hold my tongue anymore. It's over!"

Briana sighed, tired of arguing with her sister. She didn't really know what to do about her feelings, or how to calm her down. Briana had never seen such an ugly side of Tiana. Sure, when they were growing up in the house together she'd noticed some things, like when Tiana would put night time medicine in her Coke. Or, when she became best friends with the mean girls at school who didn't like her. Even when Briana would share a secret with her sister and make Tiana promise not to tell their parents, Tiana always did.

Never in a million years did Briana think Tiana would grow to hate her until now. The way her sister sounded on the other end of the phone sent shivers down her spine. She didn't even sound like the twin sister she'd always shared a room with when they were younger. She sounded like a complete stranger.

"Tell me what I can do to help you?" Briana said.

A cynical laugh escaped Tiana. "Help me?" she said with a smile as bright as the sun. "My dear sister, you are mistaken. You are the one who needs help."

A frown crossed Briana's face. "How so?" she asked.

"Let me ask you, how fast are you going in that Mini Coop of yours, huh?"

Briana looked at her speedometer; it read 83 miles an hour. "What does my speed have to do with anything?"

"That's okay, you don't have to tell me, but I know how fast you drive. Let me just say, good luck trying to stop." Tiana disconnected the call.

Briana threw her cell phone in the passenger seat and hit the brakes. They went all the way to the floor, with only air squeezing out of them. She panicked. "Oh my God!" Briana continued to slam on the brakes, but they responded only with shrieks of air.

"Jesus Christ!" Briana screamed. He was the only one who could help her right now.

Over and over again, Briana squeezed the brakes. It was no use, she got the same result. She focused on the road before her. How long could she continue to navigate the car before she had to stop? A rush of heat flushed through her. Nervousness hit the pit of her stomach.

"Oh dear God, help me!"

The car was picking up speed now. At any moment, she would run into traffic on 85 North. A silver Chevrolet Tahoe sped past her and jumped in front of her, cutting her off.

"Get out of my way!" she screamed.

The truck driver threw up his middle finger. Traffic was slowing around them. Briana glanced to the side of the highway. The treads might slow her down, but that didn't mean she would stop. It was possible that she would just go flying down the side, and that wouldn't be good either. She tried to think of another solution, but there wasn't one. She swerved out of the left lane, navigating the Mini Coop around and in front of the cars. Horns blasted her way. People were giving her a piece of their minds for cutting them off. Just when she thought she might make it, traffic slowed down even more. Her Mini Coop was the only car flying around cars, and soon the highway sounded like a chorus of horns.

The innocent people around her had no way of knowing

what was really going on. A woman in a red Toyota Camry decided to teach the impractical driver a lesson on road manners. She jumped in front of Briana and slowed to almost a stop.

Briana screamed. "AAAAAAAAAAAAA!"

Her Mini Coop banged into the back of the Toyota Camry. Her car did a double flip, and the Toyota was pushed into three other cars with such force that they all were totaled on the spot. Briana's car landed on the passenger side. Her windows busted immediately; big and small pieces of glass flew like a tornado inside the car. The Mini Coop slid down, the tread causing more damage on the vehicle. The engine caught fire, and flames roared from the hood.

When the car finally came to a stop, Briana was no longer conscious. The seat belt she wore kept her in place, while her limbs hung to the side. Blood covered her arms and face where she'd been cut up by the glass. Flames rose higher, and other drivers ran to her car.

Someone yelled, "Help me get her out!"

Two gentlemen and a lady tried unsuccessfully to get Briana out of the car.

"She's stuck," one man said. "Her legs are caught up under the dashboard."

"We have to get her out," another man said.

"It's no use. She needs the Jaws of Life to get her out of there," the lady offered.

The flames rose and all three of them moved to safety from their vengeance. Sirens blared in the background.

"The ambulance is on its way, let them help her," the lady said again.

"By the time they get here, it may be too late," the first man said.

They stepped back to the Mini Coop and reached in, pulling and tugging on Briana.

"Take off her seat belt," the second man said.

"If we do that and she falls, who's going to climb in to get her with these flames threatening to kill us all out here? Not me. She shouldn't have been going so fast in the first place. I wonder if she was drunk," the lady said.

The sirens got closer. "I think they're going to make it."

Just then, there was a sound like a crackle of fire. They let go of Briana and moved again.

"I think it's going to blow. Move out of the way!" the lady said.

Everyone watched as the flames raged and threatened to consume the car and Briana. Still unconscious, she had no way of knowing she was on the brink of death, but her mind was at ease. Either way, she wouldn't feel a thing.

# Chapter One

### *Six Months Later*

"*Jesus, be a fence all around me every day. Jesus, I want you to protect me as I travel along the way. I know you can, yes Lord. I know you will fight my battle if I just keep still. Lord, be a fence all around me every day.*"

The choir sang, clapped and moved side to side. The Sanctuary was filled with people dancing and shouting singing along with Fred Hammond's gospel hit. Justin Gable turned to look at his wife and a smile crossed his caramel masculine face as he continued to clap.

Tiana met his eyes and smiled even harder. She still hadn't gotten used to being called Briana, and it wasn't getting any easier as time went along. Being at church every Sunday was starting to get old, but Tiana made sure to treat herself by going out on Saturdays and having a good old time. It was funny that no one had suspected that she wasn't Briana, except for Taylor, Briana's sixteen-year-old daughter, and Angela Green, Briana's best friend.

As the time passed, she'd kept an eye on the pair. Her

family didn't understand why Briana would put in her notice with her job as one of the top legal associates and partners at the firm. Angela didn't understand the divide between them. They'd always shared everything, every experience, every frustration, every blessing. She could tell something was different; she just hadn't been able to put her finger on it.

Angela would come to the house and take Taylor out for what she called, auntie time. As far as Tiana was concerned, the two were up to something. Tiana's cards had been played right, but if anybody got in the way of her happiness, she would take them out. No matter who it was. It was just as easy to make an accident happen as it was to make sweet potato pie. She'd learned that first hand with Briana.

The day of her twin sister's accident was the first day of the rest of Tiana's life. With her out of the picture, she could finally be the only one with her looks walking the face of the planet. Although Briana's accident didn't necessarily see its way through, it was just a matter of time before it did. It didn't make Tiana happy that her twin didn't die in the car crash, but her being in a coma would have to be good enough for now.

No one from the hospital had tried to contact them, and for good reason. After Briana's accident, Tiana had made her way to the hospital in disguise, and hung around the waiting room. When a doctor passed by, she had called out to him.

"Excuse me, Doctor?"

"Branigan," he said.

"Yes, Doctor Branigan I, hope you don't mind me asking, but I saw the young lady being rushed in and she looked pretty banged up. Will she be okay or should I pray for her?"

"You should pray for her. I can't really tell you any more than that unless you are a family member."

"I'm just a concerned citizen, maybe I could help you find her family."

"If you can do that, it would be a miracle in itself. She was in a car crash, and the flames ate everything in it, including her personal information. We have no way of knowing who she is. Her cuts are pretty bad, and right now, she's a Jane Doe until further notice. It's nice to see good people still exist in this world, please keep her in your prayers."

Doctor Branigan had walked away, hurrying to get to his patient. That confirmation was good enough. Throughout the first three months, Tiana had checked on Briana, making sure her condition worsened and didn't get better. For a while, things had gotten complicated, but then her condition stabilized. Tiana was tired of checking in on her, but she knew it was her duty. She needed Briana to suddenly die in her sleep or it could crumble Tiana's efforts.

There was a tug on her, and she looked down at her six-year-old niece, Denise Gable.

"Yes, honey?" she asked.

"Momma, I need to go pee," Denise said.

"Okay, let's go."

Tiana grabbed her hand. "I'm taking Denise to the bathroom," she told Justin.

"Okay," he said.

They made their way down the pews past people still clapping and singing. The church was half the size of a football stadium. It would take them about ten full minutes to reach the bathroom, and another ten standing in line. Tiana kept her game face on, smiling at other brothers and sisters in Christ as she made her way through the crowd. They went up two flights of stairs before making it to the first bathroom.

Tiana pushed the door open and held it for Denise to walk through. When she released it, it swung in and out, almost tapping her on the back. Denise ran into one of the stalls and shut the door, her little legs dancing because she could no longer hold it in. Tiana pulled out her cell phone, keyed in her unlock code, and checked the three messages in her voicemail.

"What's up, this Ralph, I met you last night at the Compound. I hope you didn't forget about me because you were drunk. Give me a call back, maybe we can meet up." The phone call ended.

She pressed seven to delete the message. "Next message."

"You know I don't like talking to this voicemail. What happened to you last night? When I woke up this morning you were gone. I don't like that either, are you with me or not? Call me back."

Tiana sighed and hit one to listen to the message again. Chris was her baby. She would've loved to stay in his bed, but unfortunately, she needed to keep up appearances. Actually, she could divorce Justin and pretend to move on with her life. A smile crept around her lips. Having the power to destroy Briana's family made Tiana feel invincible, but the truth of the matter was she had grown close to the little bunch. She even had a little real love for Justin. Not to mention, the man's bed game was off the chain! No wonder Briana married him. Tiana was glad she'd got him back. He officially belonged to her anyway.

When Briana first met Justin they were at a baseball game. It was a boring Sunday afternoon and Briana had begged Tiana to come along. Giving in, Tiana went with her, both of them dressed down in jeans and a loose fitting t-shirt with high top Pumas and a baseball cap with their long hair flowing out of it. When Tiana first spotted Justin he was standing at the concession stand. She started to ignore him but then he turned slightly and their eyes met, holding her hostage in a stare down.

She remembered it like it was yesterday, her eyes had roamed the length of him, muscular arms hung out his white polo shirt, his hands tucked into the Levi jeans he wore. He gave her a smile and a wink, and in return, she blew him a kiss. As she made her way into the restroom looking for Briana, she'd thought about their little exchange and decided to be the one to make the move when she came out. Unfortunately for her, Briana had made it out the restroom first and looking just like Tiana, she'd managed to get a date with Justin.

Tiana had never forgiven her sister, but she'd never told her she had her eye on him either. Tiana never thought they'd get married and have kids, and although that was sixteen years ago, Tiana would not let it go.

"Next message."

"Hey, Bri, can we talk? I've got something I've been holding on to and I really need to have this conversation with you. Please don't tell me you don't have the time. This conversation needs to happen."

Tiana pressed seven. Angela was getting on her nerves. The girl couldn't take a hint. She really missed Briana, but Tiana couldn't care less.

Denise came out of the stall and washed her hands at the sink. She waved her hand in front of the paper towel dispenser and ripped off two sheets.

"That's a lot of paper towels for those little hands," Tiana said.

"I'm a big girl," Denise responded.

"Okay, big girl. Let's go." They went back to their seats, and by then, the pastor had started his sermon.

"Today, we're going to talk about extreme faith. It's true that you can have faith of a mustard seed and still move mountains, but if you have extreme faith, think about what you could move!"

"Yes, sir!" one man yelled.

"Any situation you come across is never too big for God.

You should never feel one ounce of worry. For what? If you have extreme faith, you know that God will supply all of your needs. I urge you today, family, put all your worries and stress on him. Ask, and you shall receive. Be a doer of the word and not just a hearer. If God be for you, who can be against you?"

"Yes!" a woman yelled.

"Good teaching," another man said.

Tiana wondered how these people could put such faith in something they had never experienced. Something they had never seen. Something they had never been able to touch, hear, or communicate with. If there was a God and he loved us the way these pastors always said, why did he make it so hard for us to communicate with him? Sounded like he was either not real or was having fun watching us get through life the best way we knew how.

Tiana shrugged. It didn't matter to her one way or the other. Surely, if God was real, he wouldn't hold it against her for not believing. With all the different religions, how could he? That would just be unfair.

"Some of you out there just have mustard seed faith. That's cool, but I challenge you today to put your faith in God and hold on firm to that faith. In due time, you'll see that extreme faith is a reality and not a fantasy."

## *Later That Day*

"Baby, Angela's at the front door for you," Justin said.

"Really? I didn't know she was stopping by." Tiana tried hard to contain her disgust.

"She used to stop by like that all the time, that's nothing new," he said.

Tiana took a sip of her margarita.

"You're drinking on a Sunday?" Justin gave her a quizzical look.

"It's just a margarita, baby, I'll be fine."

"I don't know. Should I be worried about this new habit of yours? The arm on the freezer door is lined with these little margarita pouches."

"Baby, look." She put the package in his face. "You see that? Five percent alcohol. This isn't about to do anything to me that I can't handle."

"Yeah, well, if you drink enough of those, it might."

"But I'm not. I'm only drinking one."

"Alright." He threw his hands up. "We'll finish this conversation later."

Tiana turned toward the trash can and rolled her eyes. She tossed the empty margarita pouch in the trash and picked up her wine glass. After taking another sip, she laid a soft kiss on Justin's lips.

"I love you," she said.

"I love you too."

In the living room, Angela sat with her brown legs crossed in a haltered floral pink dress that fit snugly down her waist and flared out past her hips down to her mid-calves. She had accessorized the dress with a pair of pink earrings and a necklace. Her hair hung down to her shoulders, flipped back at the edges in a Farrah Fawcett style. She gave a half smile when Tiana walked in the room.

"Did you get my voice message?"

"I did," Tiana responded.

"You didn't call me back."

"Yeah, I've been busy. I was at church in the restroom when I actually listened to the voicemail."

"Oh, well, can we take a ride?"

Tiana tried to think of a way to get out of being alone

with Angela, but for the very first time, she was at a loss for words.

"I guess, after you?" Tiana said, motioning for the door. She took another sip of her margarita.

"You're not bringing that, are you?" Angela asked.

"Maybe," Tiana said. Angela arched her eyebrows. "I'm just playing." Tiana displayed a sweet smile.

She was trying to lighten the mood because the air around them was definitely thick. Tiana put her glass in the fridge and went to find Justin. He was sitting in his man cave with the game blasting on TV.

"Hey, babe, I'll be back. About to take a ride with Angela real quick."

"Okay, come give me some love."

Tiana walked in the room and bent over him. Their kiss was long and sensual. Tiana pulled back with her eyes lowered seductively at him.

Justin felt his arousal push at the zipper of his pants. His masculine thighs tightened at the sensation. "You know the kids are going to stay at your mom's later today. She wants to take them to a movie, so we'll have the house all to ourselves," he said.

"Mmmm, what time?" Tiana asked.

Justin looked down at his watch. "In about an hour to be exact." He gave her a smirk and leaned forward to kiss her on her full lips again.

"In that case," she said, "I'll be back in thirty minutes."

As she turned to walk off, he popped her on her backside, causing her butt to bounce. She glanced back and sashayed off. The thought of her breaking up the family earlier was gone. Justin was the perfect man for her, and they would be together 'til death do them part.

Outside in the car, Angela sat with the engine running,

hoping to get something accomplished today. Her friend had completely done a one eighty, and she was not feeling the change. The thing that worried her the most is that she had been acting a lot like her twin. Angela tried not to let that bother her because twins did that all the time. However, she'd known Briana for over a decade, and she just didn't understand why after all this time she would start showing so many traits of her sister.

Angela was determined to get down to the bottom of it, but she didn't want to scare Briana off. Lately, she'd acted like their friendship didn't hold much value, and she didn't want to lose her friend.

Tiana got in the car. "How long will this take?" she asked.

The question caught Angela off guard. "Do we have a time limit? We've never had one before."

This unnerved Tiana so badly she wanted to tell Angela, *I'm not who you think I am, that's why!*

Tiana had to admit she thought it would be easier to take over Briana's life, but the fact that everyone referred to her as Briana did not exactly give her the freedom she was looking for. Just then, a crazy yet fantastic thought came to her. She would put it into practice when she returned to Justin, just to see how it might play out.

"Actually, the kids are going to my mom's in about an hour, and Justin and I would like to take advantage of the opportunity."

Angela let a soft laugh escape her. "Oh wow, I'm sorry I asked."

"Ask, and you shall receive!" Tiana stated, quoting a Bible scripture she'd heard the pastor say many times during service.

Angela shook her head up and down in agreement. "That is true. It's too bad, though, because I wanted to spend more time with you. We haven't been as close lately as we used to be. As a matter of fact, we haven't been close in a long time. Is it okay if I just be frank?"

"Of course, by all means," Tiana said, trying to imitate Briana's propriety.

"It's like ever since your sister stopped coming around, you've changed. I know you said she wanted to live her own life and do things differently for a change, but you've seemed to have picked up a lot of her characteristics."

This made Tiana curious. "Oh yeah, how so?" she asked.

"Well, you wear your hair like she used to wear it when I first met you both. You've picked up a lot of her phrases. You're going out a lot on the weekends, and you're drinking, just to name a few. What's weirder though, is the tattoo on your neck of the musical instrument she used to play. I remember when she first got the tattoo, you said you wouldn't be caught dead with one, but then you went out and got the same tattoo in the exact same spot. You know you can talk to me about anything, right?"

"Unhuh," was all Tiana said.

"Do you miss your sister, Bri? Should we contact her and see if we can come up for a visit? I thought it might be a good idea, especially since she has no family in California. Her moving all the way to the west coast away from anyone she knows is strange enough, but surely she misses you, if no one else."

Angela was too nosey for her own good, and Tiana didn't like it one bit. Tiana had the feeling Angela was going to be trouble. "I don't know if she does miss me, Angela—"

"And that's another thing," she said, cutting Tiana off. "You've always called me Angie. Why are you calling me Angela? Only my dad calls me that. If I didn't know any better, I would say either you are having a midlife crisis or you are really Tiana impersonating Briana." Angela laughed hard at her statement.

To her, it was just a joke. She didn't really think her friend was having a midlife crisis or impersonating her twin. However, Tiana didn't find it funny at all. She was so bothered by the statement her forehead started to sweat.

Tiana looked at the time on the dashboard. "Where are we going?" she asked, ignoring everything Angela had just said.

"I thought we might grab something to eat."

"I don't have an appetite," Tiana said.

Angela frowned. "I didn't smell any food coming from your kitchen. Did you eat already?"

"Actually, no, but that's another reason I should get back home."

"We've only been gone for fifteen minutes. I'm sure you could spare another thirty, right?"

Angela turned into the Waffle House and parked. Tiana opened the door and walked toward the Waffle House, happy to get out of the car. She needed all the air she could get.

Inside, there was a waitress calling out orders, and two other waitresses obviously on their breaks. They sat at a booth next to a window, looking disheveled like they'd worked a double shift. Tiana sat down in one of the swivel chairs up front.

Angela joined her. "Do you want to get a booth?" she asked.

"No, we won't have much time for that. I was thinking we would order to go. I might as well get something for Justin while I'm here."

"Get something for yourself too, you might not be hungry now, but you will be later."

The waitress walked up. "What can I get you?"

"I'll have two of your all-star breakfast combos," Tiana said.

"How do you want your eggs?"

"Scrambled with cheese, I also want raisin toast, and bacon instead of sausage for both."

The waitress finished scribbling on her order pad. "And you, ma'am?" she said.

"Yes, I'll have your pork chop and eggs," Angela said.

"Anything else?"

"That's it."

"Will this be on separate orders?"

"No, I'll take care of it," Angela said.

"No, no, I'll pay for our food. You pay for yours."

"It's no problem, I don't mind at all," Angela protested.

The waitress looked from Tiana to Angela, waiting for them to make up their mind. Tiana quickly took out her American Express card to pay for her purchase. She didn't want anything from Angela, not her money, not her conversation, and not her friendship. As far as Tiana was concerned, she could keep it all. It wasn't like they were really friends. She was someone who had always kept her nose in the air when it came to Tiana, and having to put up with her for even a moment, was longer than Tiana could stand.

The waitress walked away to put the order in.

Angela took out her MasterCard. "I guess I'll get it next time."

Tiana turned to her. "Why do you think you have to buy my food? I'm no charity case."

"I never said you were. Hey, where is all this coming from? You act like we've never paid for each other's lunch before. What is wrong with you?"

"Nothing is wrong with me, is it okay for me to pay for my own purchases?"

Angela was completely confused. Her friend was turning into the Grinch that stole Christmas right before her very eyes. "Something is wrong with you, you've changed."

"Says you. No one else seems to think so."

"Actually, your own daughter thinks so."

Tiana sat back in her chair. "And how do you figure that?"

"I talk to Taylor all the time, she calls me when she feels she can't talk to you," Angela said.

"She can talk to me anytime she wants," Tiana spat.

"That's not what she thinks. She feels disconnected from you, and she can't put her finger on it. I'm inclined to say the same."

"What are you saying, Angela? That I'm somebody else? Because the last time I checked, I'm me, my DNA is the same, my life is the same, my husband is the same, my kids are the same, my parents are the same. The only thing that's changed is my job, and maybe my friends!"

Angela was taken aback by the sting in her words. She sucked her teeth.

Tiana saw the hurt on Angela's face, so she softened her stance a bit. "Sure, I've picked up on some of my sister's traits, but we're twins, for Pete's sake. You are exaggerating, please get over it."

The waitress approached the table with their food and took Angela's payment. The girls got up and quietly left the restaurant. They returned to the car and rode to Briana's house in silence.

# Chapter Two

"She's stable, but no sign of her waking up yet. I'll tell you one thing, she's definitely a fighter. When she came in she was in really bad shape. To be honest, none of us thought she would make it this long on her own. But you never know what God is up to."

"You can say that again. I was the one who pulled her from the car. It was totaled, and her pulse was light. Someone is watching out for her."

"Were you one of the Samaritans trying to get her out?"

"Actually, I was on the job. I'm with North Brooke Fire Department. We were the first responders besides the helpful motorists. They did a good job trying to get her out, but we had to put the fire out first. I've been checking up on her every now and then, since she has no family."

"That's really nice of you."

Briana could hear voices around her, but couldn't quite make them out. Two male voices. Slowly, her eyes opened. Everything was blurry. Her body felt stiff and a little sore. With all her might, she fought to clear her eyesight. The first object she could make out was a television hanging on the wall right in front of her. The light in the room was so bright, it bore down on her eyes, making her squint. She closed her eyes and rested them for a second before trying again.

Her focus was a little stronger this time. There was a man sitting next to her, his hand on hers. *Who is he?* she wondered. From the side view of his face, he was handsome. He sat back in his chair with his leg propped up, his ankle meeting where his knee and his thigh connected. His hair was cut and shaped to the outline of his face, and small waves ripped over his head. Dark black hair on chocolate brown skin. *Does he belong to me?* she wondered.

Briana was confused. She was in a hospital; this much was obvious. But what happened to her? Her hand moved and he turned to look at her. From this angle, she hoped he belonged to her. His light brown eyes complemented his face, and she loved the little hump at the end of his strong masculine nose. She wondered if she'd ever kissed those full lips before. Before she could ask any questions, he jumped up and ran to the door.

"Nurse!" he yelled. "Nurse!" The nurse came flying in the room. "She's up!"

Immediately, the nurse called for Doctor Branigan. While they waited for the doctor, the nurse checked her pulse and vital signs.

"How long has she been up? I just left the room not ten minutes ago."

"She just opened her eyes. I think I was watching the television, but I felt her hand move."

"Her vitals are still good."

"What … happened?" Briana asked, barely able to get the words out.

"You were in a car accident."

"Oh, how long have I been here?"

The nurse looked at her friend and back to her. "Six months."

She gasped. "What?" Briana said. "Are you serious? What kind of car accident was this?"

"You don't remember?" her friend asked.

"No, and I don't remember you either."

"That's because you've never met me. My name is Charles Finnegan. I'm the firefighter who pulled you out of the car."

"I see," Briana said. She was taken aback by the concern on Charles face. He was a complete stranger, and yet he was there, and no one else was. "Where is my family?"

Charles and the nurse shared another look. "We don't know. All of your belongings were destroyed in the accident, so we didn't have a way of contacting your next of kin," the nurse said. "If you can give me your name, I can get right on it for you."

Briana thought long and hard about the question. It should've been an easy one, but unfortunately, it wasn't. "I can't remember," she said.

Doctor Branigan entered the room. "Well, look who finally decided to join us here in the real world," his baritone voice boomed. "It's very nice to see your eyes. God must have favor over you. How do you feel?"

"I feel stiff. Can I get up?"

"Well, let's start off slow for now."

"I've been here for six months. That's slow enough, isn't it? My head hurts." She tried to move and Charles rushed to her side. Their eyes connected for a long minute, Briana adoring the concern on his face like he was a long lost lover.

"That's why I want you to take it slow. You've been laying for so long, any rush to get up too soon will make you dizzy," the doctor said.

He went to her other side, and together, they helped her sit up. The nurse hit a button on the front of the bed that made the back of it rise to a sitting position. Charles took the two pillows off the bed and propped them behind her back.

"Is that comfortable?" he asked.

Never taking her eyes off of him, Briana responded, "Much better." They held each other's gaze for another long second.

"That's great," Doctor Branigan said. "Now, all we have to do is call your family and let them know you've woken up. So who's your next of kin?"

"She doesn't know," the nurse said.

The doctor looked at Briana questioningly. "You've got some memory loss. That's common with people who are in a coma for a period of time. It may take a while for you to remember anything, but don't worry, you'll have this good fella here if you need anything. I'm starting to believe he's your guardian angel. Mr. Finnegan has stood watch over you every other day for the past six months. I've never met anyone like him."

Briana gave Charles another long look, then spoke to Doctor Branigan. "Am I okay? How much longer will I have to stay in this hospital?"

"You've actually healed miraculously. Your cuts were pretty severe, but I've never seen anyone heal quite like you. We'll run a few more tests to make sure you're one hundred percent, then if everything's okay, you'll be released. But first, we need to try and locate your family or you won't have anywhere to go."

"I'll make sure she has somewhere to go if we can't locate her family," Charles said. "If that's okay with you." He turned to Briana.

Briana shook her head up and down. What other choice would she have? She wondered how she could be in the hospital for six months and no one had looked for her. Maybe she didn't have any family after all. It was sad to think that way, but how could she have loved ones who didn't come and look for her? If a family member of hers had come up missing, the first place she would look is the jail and then the hospital.

"Where are we exactly?" Briana asked.

"We're in Gwinnet County Hospital in Atlanta, Georgia."

"Do you know if I live here, or if I was visiting?"

"No, we don't, sorry," the doctor said with sadness.

Briana sighed. She didn't think anyone would come for her. If they hadn't come already, why would they come now?

## *Three Days Later*

Justin and Tiana pulled into Mary Mac's Tea room on Ponce De Leon Avenue. Bible study Wednesday always gave them a refresher course from Sunday's service and kept them going strong for the week. Tiana was getting used to the services. Although going without them would be more her taste, they did always seem to bring her and Justin closer.

"I love you," she said, squeezing his hand.

"I love you too, baby." He leaned over and planted a kiss on her rose colored lips.

They got out of the car and walked into the restaurant. Once again, Tiana's mom had the kids. It was welcomed because Tiana could only take so much of Taylor. The little brat had been acting out more and more these days. She'd actually received a call from the school saying that Taylor's grades had dropped and they wanted to set up a parent teacher conference. The last thing Tiana wanted to do was sit in the school and play concerned parent with Taylor's teachers.

Somehow, Taylor was able to tell the difference between her and Briana, and she was becoming a pain in Tiana's side. Denise, on the other hand, didn't notice a difference, and loved being around Tiana. She helped Tiana around the kitchen, always wanting to wash the dishes. When Denise had homework, Tiana was the first person she went to, and they sat down and finished it in good timing for her to eat and go to bed.

Why did teenagers have to be so difficult? Tiana wondered if she could kill her and get away with it. An accident could happen at any time. That's what she kept telling herself. The only reason one hadn't happened so far is because she knew it would put her family in turmoil. Accident or not, they would be devastated if something happened to the little brat, and Tiana didn't have the energy to go through with it. Not yet, anyway.

If Taylor kept trying her patience, Tiana might just find the energy. Or, maybe she could convince Justin to send her to boarding school. It was less drastic. Yes, she would do that. Let the little brat keep messing up, and she would give her best Hollywood performance to Justin on why they needed to send her away. If that didn't work, it was off with her head, period.

"Only two for this evening?" the waitress asked.

"Yes, just me and my lovely wife," Justin responded.

Tiana loved it when he said things like that about her. Monday, while she was at work, he'd had a bouquet of roses delivered. They were so beautiful it made Tiana's day. The only thing was the card said, *To my beautiful wife Briana, please accept these roses as a small token of my love.*

The roses were sweet, but the name Briana leapt off the note at her like a sharp knife. No matter how hard she tried, the fact that he thought she was her sister made Tiana sick to her stomach. Instantly, she snatched the note off and tossed it in the trash. The staff at her job swooned over the bouquet and talked about how good a man he was. That was something she already knew, and that made her want to hold tighter to him.

Justin pulled her chair out and Tiana sat down. He sat across from her and picked up his menu. "So how's work at Sharp Images?" he asked.

"It's going great. I've been put on more assignments than I may be able to handle, but they want their best photographer on the job for their clients, so what can I say?"

Justin gave her a sexy smile. "I'm sure you can handle it."

Tiana could gobble him up. He had definitely grown on her, and that smile made her body tingle. She tried not to think about sex. "Did it bother you when I decided to leave my job at the firm and make my hobby a full time career?"

Justin searched her concerned face. "I am happy that you found your niche. The last thing we want in life is to do something that doesn't make us happy. Still, I've been wondering why you never mentioned wanting to be a photographer before."

Tiana had trained herself for this conversation. She and Justin had never been around each other more than an hour at a time, and that was every other month or so. Seeing him made her angrier with her sister for stealing a life that could've possibly been hers, so she stayed away from them as much as possible.

"I knew how much you enjoyed practicing law together so I stuck it out. It's not that I didn't like my profession, it just wasn't my first love. Photography is."

"It seems I'm learning new things about you every day," he said.

"Angela seems to think it's out of my character. She makes it seem like I'm not the person I've always been."

Justin chuckled. "And what do you think about that?" He lifted his glass of water and took a sip.

"I think she's a little jealous, if you ask me."

"She's always been a good friend, and I'm sure she means no harm. But sometimes when people do better in life, it does bring out the jealously in others. What did you tell her?"

"That I'm the same person I've always been, and she should stop tripping."

Justin laughed again.

What's so funny?" Tiana asked.

"I like the way you drop the proper speech sometimes and give me that sister girl talk."

They both laughed.

"You've been very supportive of me, and you like a lot of things I've done differently, even in the bedroom. I didn't know you didn't like the things I did before."

"I didn't say that. I loved the things you did before, or I wouldn't have married you. But every marriage could use a spark or things can get stale, and you've sparked it up for sure."

"I have a feeling you're referring to Sunday night."

"Not just Sunday night, but that was very different. I didn't know you had it in you. Let me be totally honest, I was conflicted with your request. I have to ask why would you want such a thing? It's almost sinful."

When Tiana had returned from her awkward luncheon with Angela, she'd gone into the bathroom and pulled out a sexy lingerie piece that she'd picked up from Fredrick's of Hollywood over the weekend. When she came out, she went downstairs to his man cave and found Justin screaming at the game. When he turned toward her, she saw the lust in his eyes. He sat up straight and turned down the television.

"I have an idea," she said.

"I'm all ears," he responded.

"Let's have some unique fun tonight."

He gave her that same sexy smile. "Okay, by unique, you mean…"

Slowly and seductively she walked to him. "I want to pretend I'm someone else."

Justin raised an eyebrow.

Tiana bent over him. "I want you to spank me and call me Tiana," she said.

Justin was shocked by this revelation. "I don't know if that's a good idea."

Tiana pouted. "Why not?"

"Because, baby, you don't think that would make you feel uncomfortable?"

"If I thought that, I wouldn't have asked you to do it."

She loosened the tie around his neck and unbuttoned his shirt. He helped Tiana as she pulled off his clothes, then she pushed him back down in the chair. "Now do as mommie asked you to do." Her voice dipped low and sultry.

Justin was still unsure until Tiana got down between his legs and took matters into her own hands. His head dropped back and he'd called her Tiana throughout the night. She couldn't get enough of it, and once pleasure overtook him, he didn't seem to care one way or the other. But the next day it had bothered him extensively.

"What's gotten into you lately?" he asked.

Tiana thought quickly. She was not prepared for this particular question because the decision was made on impulse. "You didn't seem to think so at the time."

Justin's eyebrow rose. "Actually, I did, I just ended up getting distracted." He gave her a stern look.

"It's like you said, baby, I just wanted to spice things up." She smirked and turned her cell phone on. It beeped, indicating a voicemail.

"I'd rather not do that again. It was really out of character. I don't want you to completely change, woman." He half joked. "I think that was crossing a line that shouldn't have been crossed. I had to repent after that session."

Tiana giggled and Justin grinned. "Let me ask you this. The going out on Saturdays and drinking you're doing, is that just a phase or what?"

"The last time I checked I was a grown woman, Justin."

"A grown married woman with two kids at home," he countered. "I know a woman should have her 'me' time and a ladies' night out every now and then, but it is becoming a pattern. What's up? Talk to me."

Tiana sighed. "If it makes you feel any better I'll cut out the drinking and slow down on going out."

It didn't go over with her too well, but she needed to do what she had to. All the questions were starting to trouble her.

"Yes, that would be much better. I need you at home in bed with me, woman. You know we've got to be on time for church."

Tiana didn't respond. With her cell phone in hand, she pressed one and waited for the voicemail to ring. "One new message."

"Hi, Michelle, this is Doctor Branigan at Gwinnett County Hospital. Good news, our patient has woken up and your prayers have been answered. You can come see her anytime. I told her about your kindness and she's looking forward to meeting you. Right now, she has slight memory loss, and we are going to run some tests to see how bad the damage is. Just thought I would let you know. Have a good night."

# Chapter Three

"Let me help you out. Hold on."

Charles Finnegan jumped out of the driver's seat of his Dodge Durango and ran around to the passenger side to open Briana's door. A week had passed since she first woke from her slumber, and there was still no sign of her family. Unable to remember who she was had definitely made the choice for her to leave with Charles. He seemed to be the kindest gentleman, and to assure her that he wasn't crazy, Charles allowed a criminal background check to be done and brought to the hospital.

After everyone was satisfied with his clean background, she was released into his care. Doctor Branigan suggested that Charles not leave her alone for a while. It was no problem for him. As he helped her to the door, they had no way of knowing they were being watched. Charles stuck his keys in the door and opened it, allowing Briana to step over the threshold.

Cinnamon scents played with her nose as she got a view of the living area. A gray shaggy rug outlined the floor in front of a black sectional couch accented with white and gray pillows. A fifty-inch flat screen TV sat on the wall. It looked to be brand new. The walls were a light gray and black.

"I'll show you to your room," he said.

Briana followed him down a long hallway to a guest bedroom. The colors in this room were red and white; everything accented and complimented the space. The king sized bed was huge, and she wondered where he got his taste.

"After you finish getting comfortable in here, I'll show you the rest of the house," he said.

"Thank you," she responded.

"I meant to ask, what would you like me to call you?"

"I told the doctors Gabrielle," Briana said.

"Nice, Gabrielle what?" he asked.

With hesitation, she said, "Finnegan."

Charles' eyebrows lifted.

"I couldn't think of anything else," Briana said. "Sorry."

His lips curved into a lazy smile. "Is that right?"

He stood tall, placing his hands inside his jean pockets.

Briana hunched her shoulders in embarrassment.

"Okay, Gabrielle… Finnegan," he said, his smile getting brighter by the minute. "I'll be downstairs if you need me." He stood there taking in her features as if he was seeing her for the first time. Her eyes, sexy and slanted slightly on the edges, her lashes, long and curvy. And that wasn't the only thing curvy about her.

He turned and left the room as she checked out his butt and smirked. Briana walked around, admiring the curtains, dresser and closet space. The clock on the nightstand read three o'clock p.m. With the sway of her hand, she pulled the curtain back and looked out the window. The house next to his looked like it sat on its own plantation. There was so much yard, and already, she could tell he'd bought the house as if he had a full family to fit inside it.

Her eyes darted across the street and she noticed a black Lexus sitting at the corner. At most, she could tell there was someone inside, but she couldn't make out what they were doing. Maybe they were waiting for someone, maybe they were on the phone. She had witnessed Charles pull over when he wanted to send a text, maybe that's what they were doing. She closed the curtain.

There wasn't any luggage for her to unpack, there was no purse for her to carry or put up. There was nothing. With the absence of her memory, she felt like nobody. No background, no roots, no nothing. The thought had crossed her mind that she could go to the police station and have her fingerprints ran. But the more she thought about it, she decided that maybe she'd lost her memory for a reason. What if she was a horrible person? Why else would her family not visit her and no one show up to claim her.

Worse, what if she was wanted by the police? That would be just her luck. With her current circumstances, maybe she should just leave it alone. She stood in the mirror and studied her reflection, trying to jog a memory, any memory of her former life. After more than two minutes, she became frustrated and sat down on the bed.

"Who am I?" she said aloud.

She prayed to God that she would find out. All she wanted was to know herself. There was a soft knock at the door.

Briana rose. "Yes?"

"May I come in?" Charles asked.

"Sure, this is your house," she said.

The door opened. "But this is your space. As long as you're here, I'll always knock."

She smiled. *At least someone cares for me,* she thought.

"When you're ready, I'll be in the kitchen."

"I'm ready now," she said, then stood and walked toward him.

He opened the door and let her brush past him. When she did, they were so close, her chest touched his. She could feel the heat emanating from him. "Excuse me," she said.

"You're okay," he said, facing her.

She stood in front of him, still and unmoving. Their eyes danced over each other. From the moment he pulled her out of the mangled car, he'd thought she was beautiful, cuts and all. He wondered if she'd been on the phone or if someone had cut her off. You never knew in Atlanta. Now standing before her staring into her dark brown eyes, she was more beautiful than ever. Her hair was pinned up in a ponytail, and she still wore hospital clothes since there were none for her to put on. The innocence on her face made him wonder who she really was, and if it was possible she'd been in that accident so their paths could cross. The chemistry between them, was there, no doubt about it.

Briana cleared her throat, and for the first time since she'd walked up on him, they blinked and started to move again. Charles shut the door and she continued past him. He followed her to the front where she assumed the kitchen was.

"Are you hungry?" he asked.

"A little," she said.

"The kitchen is this way." He took the lead.

She followed him and admired the strength of his walk. Only a man would walk like that, and he had a nice butt too. She giggled and covered her mouth with her hand.

Charles looked back at her. "What's so funny?" he asked.

She shook her head vibrantly. "Nothing."

"It must be something, because you're laughing. Now, are you going to leave me hanging?"

She giggled some more. "Nice butt," she said.

"You think so?" He wiggled his eyebrows.

"Yeah, I do."

"Beautiful smile," he said.

"Thank you." She blushed.

In the kitchen, he made stir fry vegetables and chicken, adding rice as their side. "Do you like sweet tea?" he asked.

"Maybe, I'm not sure."

"If you don't, you'll love mine." Charles poured her a glass of sweet tea and added a lemon and a straw. "How do you feel?"

"Like I'm from another planet."

"Why is that?"

"Because the only thing I know for certain is that I look like everyone else. Human, I mean. I can't imagine that when people have memory loss it's a full loss like this."

"Some people do, and some people can remember things from their past. It depends on the circumstance and the reason behind the memory loss. Your accident was bad. You were lucky to wake up from that coma."

"You're right, I shouldn't be feeling sorry for myself. Excuse me."

"That's normal. I'm sure you'll have more questions and things on your mind as time goes along. We'll deal with them as they come. Do you mind if we say grace before we eat?"

Briana was in lust with him. She could tell by his words that he was not the average guy. "No, not at all," she said.

They bowed their heads and Charles spoke to the Lord. He asked for protection, guidance, and blessings over their food. While he prayed, Briana watched him. He was so handsome and had such a loving nature. Could it have been possible for them to meet on such an awkward occasion by fate? Whatever the reason, she was glad God had put her in good hands.

"In Jesus name, Amen."

"Amen," she said.

"I can say I remember him," she said.

"Who?"

"Jesus."

"And that's really all that matters," he responded.

"So you're a Christian man, huh?"

"I try to be."

"No wife or kids?"

Charles put his fork down. "They died, two years ago."

The revelation gave her pause. "I'm sorry," she said.

"For what? It wasn't your fault."

"I'm sorry for asking. Just noticing this big house and not having any family here made me curious."

"As you should be. We never lived in this house. This was one of the houses we'd picked out while house hunting. Really, we were just doing it for fun. At the time, we didn't have the financial means to own a home, with us trying take care of our family, which was getting bigger. She was pregnant. Seven months."

He hesitated.

Briana reached across the table and grabbed his hand. "Maybe we should change the subject," she said.

"Nah, I want you to know. That way, we can get it out and never have to bring it up again." He continued, "We were coming from my oldest son's birthday party that my parents had thrown him at their home. He was turning eight. We needed to pick up groceries before we went home, so we went to the party in separate vehicles to have room for the food. I drove our pick-up truck while she drove the kids in our car in front of me. The car was full. My two sons, Alex and Seth, my wife, my niece, and oldest nephew.

"Halfway to the store, a drunk driver crossed the lanes and ran into them head on. I was about two cars behind them by then. Immediately, the car went up in flames. When I got to them, I pulled over and tried to get them out, but the doors were jammed. I couldn't save them. Not one of them. I had to watch them burn. Their screams and cries." He paused again and closed his eyes, his jaws clenched.

"My God," Briana said.

His eyes glistened with fresh tears threatening to descend down his face as he relived the horrific accident.

Briana got up from the table and went to him. At that moment, boundaries were not thought of as she reached to console him. She pulled at his chair and he allowed her to comfort him. In his lap, she sat and held him as he breathed heavily into her neck, fighting back the breakdown that tried to consume him.

"The memory still hurts," he said.

"I am so sorry I asked," Briana whispered. "Please, let's change the subject. Are you okay?"

"I was able to save you," he said, his voice tight. "Ever since that day, I have devoted my time to saving people in similar situations. No family should ever have to watch a loved one die that way."

Briana felt chills flow through her. This had to be the reason he was so caring when it came to her. He truly was her guardian angel.

"I'm okay. How are you?" he asked.

"I was better before I opened my big mouth," she said.

His honey brown eyes searched hers. Charles felt her sincerity, and raw emotion ran through his gut. He was aware of her warm, soft, body invading his space, and he didn't mind it one bit. His lips met hers and they kissed. A simple kiss at first, then his hands wrapped around her waist and their kiss deepened. He turned her toward him and she straddled his lap. They kissed like long lost lovers, his lips sucking the bottom and top of her lips before inserting his tongue in her mouth.

Briana's stomach was in knots and she savored the taste of him. A moan left her mouth and found its way down Charles throat, which was met with his own barbaric, sexually stimulated grunt. As Briana slightly pulled away from him for air, Charles rained kisses down her chin, across her face and to her neck. Briana felt his arousal grow beneath her, which made her body heat up from the bottom of her toes to the top of her ears.

In a breathless voice, Briana spoke. "Maybe we should slow down."

After she said it, she regretted it. No way did she want to slow down, at least that's what her body told her. Charles' fervent kisses slowed, but didn't completely stop. Briana had set his emotions on high, and every loin in his body wanted her right then and right now. Slowly, he sat back, his broad shoulders and chest heaving, forcing himself to comply with her wishes.

"That wasn't very Christ like, now was it?" Charles said with little amusement.

Briana fidgeted. "It's just that..." She searched for the right words to say. "I don't want our lovemaking to be in vain. I don't want it to happen because you're feeling vulnerable right now."

Charles regarded her for a long moment, his thick eyelashes hovering over his strong penetrating gaze. His tongue swept across his bottom lip as he assessed her, tasting the sweetness she'd left lingering on his mouth.

"I can assure you," he said, his voice deep and husky, "when we do make love, there will be nothing vain about it."

Briana's breathing quickened. She stood, and her breast rubbed against his face. Before he could stop himself, his hands griped her waist and he stood, picking her up. Her legs instantly wrapped around him. With one arm, he pushed his dinner plate off the table, sending it crashing to the floor. Charles laid her down on the table, pressing his body against hers.

There was a momentary second of pause, just long enough to give her a chance to stop him. When she didn't, he leaned down and planted a trail of kisses from her navel up her bare, flat, stomach, to the cleft between her breasts.

"Wait," she said. It was barely above a whisper.

He groaned.

"I'm sorry."

Once again, she was assaulted by his gaze.

"It's not that I don't want to..." her voice trailed off.

He stood, letting her legs fall from his waist. He took a step back.

"No," he said. "I'm sorry, I got carried away."

Briana sat up, her body still yearning for him to forget everything she said and have his way with her. Instead, he held out his hand and helped her off the table, pulling her into his arms.

"Have a drink with me."

"Sure," she said. "Are you trying to get me drunk now?"

He gave her a half smile. "When you're ready, I won't have to get you drunk, trust me."

She smiled with thoughts of what the future could hold with this handsome man. "I don't know whether to be scared or relived."

"A little bit of both," he said.

# Chapter Four

Tiana was paranoid. It had almost turned her insane when she received that voicemail. *How in the world could Briana have woken up?* Tiana was still trying to figure it out. There was no way Briana should still be alive. Doctor Branigan had shattered her dreams with that voicemail. For the rest of the night, she didn't hear anything Justin said. She was so distracted that he asked her if she was okay. The change was that noticeable.

Tiana had gone from being calm and flirtatious to being panicked and jumpy. As it was right now, the doctor said Briana had memory loss, but how long would that last? The last thing she needed was for her to get her memory back because the truth would set her free. It would expose what a lying, backstabbing, murderer Tiana was. It would take her life away in more ways than one. Tiana couldn't have it.

The man Briana was playing house with would only appease her until that memory came soaring back, and then she might be out for revenge. Tiana shook that last thought. Her sister was many things, but vengeful was not one of them. She was a true Christian, and wouldn't put up a fight with anyone under any circumstances. That still didn't mean she wouldn't destroy everything Tiana had built.

A plan brewed in her mind. Tiana would keep a close watch on Briana, and as soon as the opportunity presented itself, she would pounce again. And this time, there would be no mistakes. Sitting with her legs crossed in Briana's bed, Tiana stroked a few keys on her laptop.

Her phone rang back to back; she'd forgotten to pick Taylor up from school. Taylor was still acting out, she'd been given after school suspension for talking back to the teacher and refusing to do her work. While she was becoming more and more out of control, the situation with Briana would have to be dealt with first. Or maybe she could kill two birds with one stone. A text message came through her phone.

***Hey love, I've been thinking about you all day. I think it's time we went on a romantic getaway,*** Justin wrote.

She replied, ***What do you have in mind?***

***How about a week in Barbados?***

***Seriously, isn't that a little expensive?***

***Nothing's too expensive for my girl.***

Tiana stared at the text without blinking. Justin treated her like a queen. As the days went on, she found herself not wanting to live without him. Denise and Justin were the only two in her life right now who were simple and loving. Even her mom was giving her strange vibes. If Tiana didn't know any better, she would swear her mom knew she wasn't Briana. This is why Tiana stayed out of her way. They'd bumped into each other once, and her mother had watched her like a hawk, assessing her movement, her talk and her attitude. If her dad ever got close enough to her, he would definitely know she was Tiana.

Her mother had sent her a message through Taylor, saying that she wanted to have lunch, but Tiana had come up with every excuse in the book not to have lunch with her mother. If her mother was able to evaluate her, she would put two and two together, and her cover would be blown.

*So, what do you say?* Justin's text message read.

*Just say when,* Tiana responded.

***In two weeks. I'll put in vacation time and we'll go. I'll ask Terri if she'll watch the kids. Love you.***

***I love you too, babe,*** Tiana responded.

The front door slammed. Tiana crawled out of bed and went toward the footsteps stomping up the stairs. To her dismay, Taylor rounded the corner. Tiana reached out to her, but Taylor pushed past her and went into her room, slamming the door. Tiana wanted to wring the little girl's neck as she followed her into her room.

"You're supposed to knock before you enter my room!" Taylor yelled.

"Excuse me, you better watch your tone. Who do you think you're talking to?"

"You are supposed to knock first! Or didn't you know that, MOM?"

Tiana's eyebrows rose. "The last time I checked, this was my house, and you don't run nothing around here. Now keep on with that tone, and get slapped back into last week."

Taylor looked horrified at Tiana's threat.

"Now what's your problem?" Tiana said.

Tears fell from Taylor's eyes. "I miss my mom!"

"What are you talking about? I am your mom, and I've been right here the whole time."

"Oh yeah? Well, you don't act like it!"

"Why do you think that?"

"We used to have girls' night twice a week, where we would stay in, pick a movie, get popcorn, sodas and candy, but you don't even mention it anymore. You forget to pick me up from school, like you don't even have a child, and what's up with the tattoo?"

Tiana tried hard not to roll her eyes. If one more person asked about that tattoo she would scream. "Okay, so I forgot to pick you up from school one time. Are you going to sue me?"

"One time? How about all this week! Who are you? You don't pay attention to us anymore, and even though Denise doesn't say anything about it, she still notices. We talk among ourselves."

"What you should've done was talk to me. I see you're talking to everyone but me."

"Who is everyone?"

"I know you've been talking to Angela, she told me. I'm sorry I haven't paid much attention to you lately. I've had a lot of things on my mind."

"Like what? What you're going to wear the next time you go out?" Taylor said with her arms crossed.

"Now, you need to mind your own business. You're pushing it, little girl, and unless you want to be on punishment, I suggest you change your attitude."

"I'll change my attitude when you change yours." Taylor rolled her eyes and turned her back on Tiana.

Three steps across the room and Tiana was in Taylor's face. She swiveled the chair around and smacked her.

"Aaah!" Taylor yelled.

"Listen here, heifer. I'm trying to be nice to you, but you're pushing it. Don't make me hurt you because I will."

The look on Tiana's face was evil. She no longer cared what Taylor thought. It was her way or no way, and she meant business.

Taylor cried and held her face. She sprang up from the chair and pushed past Tiana, running to find her daddy.

Tiana sucked her teeth, folded her arms, and strolled to the balcony. She watched Taylor run down the steps. "If you're looking for your daddy, he's not here. It's just you and me, so why don't you bring your butt back up these stairs because I'm not done with you yet!"

Taylor stopped in her tracks and looked up at Tiana. "I hate you! You're not my mother, you are a monster!"

"Yeah, well I hate you too," Tiana responded.

Taylor gasped and tears welled up in her eyes. She ran out of the house crying, leaving the door open.

Tiana rolled her eyes and sighed. She dialed Justin's phone and he picked up on the second ring.

"Hey, love, I'm on my way home now."

With fake tears, she wailed, "Honey! Taylor has gone crazy, she needs help!"

"What's wrong?" he asked.

"She seems to think I don't pay her and Denise any attention anymore, and I don't know where she's getting this from. Her grades have dropped in school, and she told me she hated me!" Tiana pretended to cry. "I'm an awful mother. How did I not see this in my own child?"

"Calm down, baby, you're not an awful mother. Taylor loves you, she's just going through her teenage phase, that's all. I'll talk to her when I get there."

"No, you don't understand, she called me a heifer and tried to slap me! Then she said she would call the police and tell them I slapped her!"

"WHAT?" He was outraged. "Hold on, I'm pulling in the driveway now!"

Tiana ended the call and put on her best sad face. With him there, she had to force the tears to flow, and now her acting skills would really be put into practice. With the door still open, Justin walked in.

"Where is she?"

"I don't know," Tiana said. "She ran out the door. I think I saw her get in the car with some guy."

Justin turned around and went back outside to see if he could spot Taylor. He took out his cell phone and dialed her cell. The only reason she had one was for emergencies, and this was one of those times.

"Daddy! Are you home?"

"Where are you?"

"I'm at Jessica's house down the street," Taylor sniffled.

"Don't lie to me, young lady. Are you with some boy?"

"No, Daddy, I promise!"

"Get home right now! You've got sixty seconds!" He disconnected the call.

Justin went back in the house and up the stairs to find Tiana. She lay across the bed, crying the best tears she could.

"Heyyy, come here, baby. Everything is going to be okay. I'll put an end to this, don't worry."

"She hates me, Justin, her own mother." Tiana pretended to cry harder.

Justin consoled her as the front door opened and closed.

"I'll be right back," Justin said.

He went to the balcony. Taylor rushed to him and threw her arms around him. She cried with her head in his chest.

"Exactly what are you crying for?" he asked.

"She slapped me and told me she hated me!" Taylor said, pointing to Tiana.

Tiana wailed dramatically and buried her face in her hands.

Justin pulled away from Taylor and kneeled down in front of her. "Taylor, what has gotten into you? Didn't I raise you to tell the truth and do the right thing? Why are you being so hard on your mom? Even if she has been a little unfocused, it's no reason to lie on her or try to put your hands on her. Now,

I'm very disappointed in you. You're grounded for a month, and you'll do your chores and Denise's while on punishment. Don't you ever let me find out you're calling your mom heifers and trying to fight her ever again, young lady, do you hear me!"

Taylor's world came crashing down. She felt a sting of betrayal like no other as she ran to her room and slammed the door. Justin felt bad about this whole ordeal. He was certain Taylor was just going through a phase. He had no way of knowing his 'wife' was really an intruder in his home, and that her primary focus was to destroy anyone and everyone who made her job harder.

There was a knock at the front door. While Tiana continued her performance, Justin went to the door and looked out the window. It was Terri, his mother-in-law.

"Hi, Terri."

"Good evening," she said. "I guess you didn't get a chance to pick Denise up, so I'm bringing her home. Everything okay?"

"Yeah, everything's fine. Taylor is having some problems in school and she's starting to act out more. I'm a little worried, but I'll keep a close eye on her."

"Ah yes, it's that time. Don't hold your breath, though, it might get a little worse before it gets better. The thing that will get you is when she starts smelling herself. Then she'll think she can do what she wants and nobody can tell her anything. She'll demand more freedom, and she'll talk about how she's almost grown. Oh yeah, it'll go on and on, maybe even until she gets out on her own and has to really fend for herself. Then, all things will come into perspective and she'll be calling to see if she can get help paying her rent."

Terri and Justin chuckled. He hugged Denise.

"Has she eaten?"

"Yeah, spaghetti. Do you want me to talk to Taylor?"

"Not tonight," he said.

"Where's my daughter?" she asked.

"Upstairs."

"Do you mind telling her to come down so I can speak to her, since I can't get her to meet me for lunch?"

"You know I would, but I don't think right now is a good time."

"Why not?"

"Her and Taylor are having some problems, and she's not in the best of moods."

"I see." Terri wanted to get down to the bottom of this. "Well, tell her I came by, and to call me soon or I'll show up at that so called job of hers and then she won't have a choice."

"So called job?" Justin questioned.

"Yeah, I said it. Gone quit her job as a partner and go take some silly photos. I don't know what has gotten into her. Sounds like something her sister would do."

"It's what she loves to do. There's nothing wrong with that."

"Yeah, if it was paying her what she was getting paid to do at the firm. I'm sure it's not nearly as much."

"I wouldn't be so sure, but I hear you." Justin wanted to wrap this conversation up so he could get back to his wife.

"Come give Grandma some sugar, sweetie."

Denise hopped down off the couch and went to her grandmother.

"Alright, I'll see you this weekend, okay."

"Okay, bye Granny."

"Bye, baby. I'll see you later, Justin."

"Be safe, and call me when you've made it home. I'm sorry you had to come out."

"No problem."

"Young lady," Justin said after Terri walked out the door. "Are you hungry?"

"No, Daddy. Can I watch SpongeBob?"

"For a little while, but then you'll be going to bed."

"Okay."

Justin took two steps at a time back to the bedroom. Tiana lay across the bed with her face in the pillows. Justin crawled in behind her, cuddled her in his arms, and kissed softly on her neck, shoulders, and back.

"I love you," he said.

Tiana lay her face to the side. "I love you too," she said. "But, baby, what if this gets worse? We may have to send Taylor to boarding school or something." Tiana shuddered, like the thought of sending Taylor away was frightening.

Justin thought about what his mother-in-law had just said. "Before we take any measures like that, we will do our duties as parents and make sure she's in line. I won't allow her or any other child to disrespect you."

"Taylor will just think we're against her," Tiana said.

"I know, baby, I know, but we'll do what we have to do."

# Chapter Five

*North Brooke Fire Department*
*Central Fire Station*

"Well, that's something I haven't seen in a long time."

Charles looked up. "What's that?"

"That silly school boy grin plastered all over your face."

Charles' smile widened. "What, no come back?" Chief Richardson said. "Now I know I'm missing something. Who's responsible?"

At that moment, David Blake entered the room. "Hey, Finnegan."

He walked to the refrigerator and pulled out a bottle of water and leaned against the door. "What ever happened to that woman you were going to visit at the hospital? Did she make it?"

"Sure did," Charles answered.

"Oh, that's God right there," David said.

"You're talking about the one on 265 with the Mini Coop?" Chief Richardson asked.

"Yeah," David said. "I told my wife about it, and you know

my wife prays for everybody, so you can believe she was praying for her. What was her name again?"

"Gabrielle."

"Nice," David said. "How she doing?"

"Really good, man, she's out of the hospital and thriving."

"Is that so?"

"Yeah."

Blake looked from Chief Richardson back to Charles. "Did I interrupt something?" he asked?

"I was just asking Finnegan here what's the school boy grin on his face about, but he hasn't answered me yet."

Charles took a sip of his Coke, not saying a word.

"Well?" David asked.

"Well, what?" Charles said.

"Are you going to answer the man?"

"Hadn't planned on it," Charles said.

The door to the kitchen opened, and in walked another one of the firemen, Alonso Blackwood.

"Finnegan, you've got a visitor, man."

He stepped aside, and all eyes went to Briana. Her smile was timid and genuine.

"I brought you lunch." She raïsed a picnic basket in the air. "That's, of course, if you haven't eaten already."

Her voice was sultry and feminine, but soft at the same time. The men eyed her, moving from her dark almond shaped eyes, to her slim nose, down to the ebony curls that surrounded her shoulders. Charles' smile was from ear to ear now, showing pearly white teeth with a twinkle in his eye. This woman was so gorgeous, and her attitude made her one of a kind.

"Today's my lucky day then," Charles said. The men turned to him. "Fellas, this is Gabrielle..." He paused for dramatic effect, then said, "Finnegan."

The men eyes grew large. They turned from Charles back to Briana.

"Wait, what did I miss?" Chief Richardson said.

"Did you get married, Finnegan?" Blake asked.

The smile on Charles face was undeniably sexy, and Briana was blushing so hard her cheeks were about to fall off.

"It's a long story," Charles said, wanting to save her from their questioning glances.

"We got time," the men said in unison.

"We don't." Charles tossed the Coke into the trash. He sauntered over to Briana, coming so close, she thought he would lean in for a kiss. "Lunch, huh?" he said.

"Yeah." A sweet carefree smile brightened her face.

Briana watched as his eyes lowered to her mouth then slowly moved back to her eyes. He was so handsome, all that chocolate coated skin and those sexy eyes that roamed freely over her. Those full lips summoning her to taste them. She wanted him to kiss her, but she wouldn't say that. She loved the way his shape up outlined his short cut hair, but he topped it off with that sexy goatee that ended in a small beard. Someone cleared their throat.

"I'll be back soon, fellas," Charles said without turning around.

He placed his hand at the small of her back and led her out. Blake and Chief Richardson were still stuck on Briana's last name being Finnegan, and if Charles thought he'd gotten away from being grilled, he could guess again.

Charles opened the passenger door to his Dodge Durango and helped Briana in. Once inside, she let out a slow, but much needed breath. Being around Charles was so exhilarating. Her pulse always quickened and she constantly felt like a little girl with a crush. Why did he make her so tense? How is it that she could feel so strongly about him, and she didn't even really know him?

Briana set the basket in the back and relaxed into the seat. Her arm rested casually on the armrest as her eyes followed him around the car to the driver's side. Once in, he turned the ignition, put the car into gear and relaxed his arm. It grazed hers, and the small fine hair on her arm stood up, sending shivers up her shoulders and down her spine. Her mouth parted, letting out the softest sound.

It didn't go unnoticed. He side eyed her then turned full circle to look at her.

"Thank you for bringing me lunch. That was sweet." His voice was deep and smooth as he gave her a half smile and winked.

Briana's words were caught in her throat and she didn't say a word. She couldn't speak, but the goosebumps that rose up her arm told their own story.

Charles pulled off and headed toward Sumner Park. Briana turned to look out the window. She could use a distraction, if only for a moment.

This area of town was very homey. Lots of trees covered the area, along with schools and playgrounds. Some of the houses they passed were gorgeous and fit for a queen. She let her mind wander with thoughts of a Victorian house filled with her and Charles' children. She watched as they opened up presents on Christmas Eve. "Just one gift can be opened tonight," she heard herself saying as Charles leaned against the wall in the entryway with a proud look on his face.

"What's on your mind, sweetheart?" she heard Charles say.

Immediately, her face lit up fire engine red. How embarrassed she was at the silly thoughts entertaining her mind.

"Must've been good, 'cause I've been watching you this whole time, and not once have you blinked."

Briana turned to him. She didn't know if she was more turned on by the fact that he'd been watching her, or by the look on his face now. If she was a meal, she was sure he would eat her up.

"Actually," she said, "I was thinking about how good the homemade chicken pot pie is that I packed for our lunch, and how much you're going to love it," she teased.

He grinned. "Liar."

Her cheeks flamed again, and although her skin was brown, he could see the beet red on her face. "Liar, liar, pants on fire," he joked.

Briana giggled. Her pants were actually about to be on fire if she didn't cool off, and soon.

He turned into the park entrance and found a quick spot. Jumping out of the car, he took long strides to the passenger door and opened it. He left just enough room for her to stand without touching him. It didn't really matter because they were so close she could smell his scent, which taunted her with fragrance notes of Old Spice and honey.

"Gabrielle," he said. She looked up at him expectantly. "Do I make you nervous?"

She smiled and let out a small sigh. "Yes."

He grabbed her hand, intertwining their fingers. "I wouldn't do anything to you that you didn't want. You do know that, right?" His fingers tightened around hers and he rested his arm on the top of the truck, making her stand face to face with him.

"Yes," she said, just above a whisper.

"Do you trust me?" he asked.

"Yes," she said.

He reached for her and caressed her face. Her eyes closed then slightly opened. He was a sight for sore eyes, and it was a freak accident that had him single. Yeah, she trusted him, even though she didn't trust herself. However, if he asked her to put on a blindfold and walk the plank, she would be sure to do so, knowing in her heart of hearts that he wouldn't let her fall.

"So beautiful," he said.

"I can say the same about you," she replied.

His eyes faltered and lowered to her mouth again.

"Kiss me," she said, without realizing she'd spoken the words aloud.

Without a moment of hesitation, he kissed her lips. She tasted of sweet strawberries. His hand wrapped around the back of her neck as he pulled her closer to him and deepened the kiss. He sucked the bottom of her lip and stuck his tongue down her throat. She moaned as they kissed, and what little gap that was left between them diminished as their bodies pressed against each other. ***Lord have mercy, I can't get enough of this man***, she thought.

A breeze flew around and underneath them, wrapping them in a tight embrace. She kept up with his pace and he hungrily tasted every part of her mouth. Someone nearby whistled, and Briana's eyes flew open. She noticed Charles' eyes had been open the whole time. He continued to kiss her, paying the passerby no mind. She placed her hand in the center of his chest, in an attempt to slow him down. He took the hint and slowed his pace, still nibbling on the sides of her lips and chin.

They breathed heavily into each other's lips. The heat from their mouths sent tingles through both of them. Charles could do this all day, but he had to get back to work. If he wasn't careful, he'd skip out on lunch and Briana would be his meal.

She gave him a gentle kiss on his face.

"Maybe we should find somewhere to eat before you have to be back," Briana said.

Charles was still stuck in that moment. His penetrating

eyes could pierce any woman's soul. Slowly, he licked his lips and took a step back. Briana turned her back to him and bent over the seat to grab the picnic basket. Charles admired her shapely figure and long legs. He thought about them being wrapped around his waist. She tilted on her toes to reach for the basket, and he took it upon himself to unlock the back door and grab the basket for her. He could only take so much. His libido was turned up, and he needed to get a hold of himself before he ended up making love to her in the truck.

Even after they'd left the car, his mind was racing with ungodly thoughts of her beneath him. This time it was Briana who tightened the hold on his hand, bringing his mind back to the here and now.

They found a spot under a huge rain tree. Briana pulled a thin blanket, a family size chicken pot pie, forks, a butter knife and glass plates from the basket. "Oh, I left the lemonade in the car," she said and stood.

"I'll grab it," Charles said, bringing her back down to her knees.

"Thanks," she said. She scrutinized his walk. "I can look at him walk anytime," she said to herself. "I've got to stop talking out loud. Now here I am talking to myself, and if anybody's watching, they're going to think I'm cuckoo for Coco Puffs."

She rearranged the dishes, cut slices and put them on both of their plates. She took out drinking glasses and sat Indian style, waiting for him to come back. As she waited, she let her tongue roam across her teeth, and checked out her dress. She tugged at it, making sure she looked nice and neat. If she'd have had a mind to, she would've brought her makeup bag, then she could check her reflection. But the last time she looked in the mirror, she was sharp. Didn't mean a hair or two wasn't misplaced now, but she wouldn't bother herself so bad about it. Briana raised her hand to her mouth and blew to smell her breath.

"Smells like strawberries," Charles said, coming up behind her.

Once again, she'd been caught being girly, and her cheeks turned beet red. "You're going to have to stop doing that," she said.

"Why? I like sneaking up on you."

"Yeah, but one day you're going to scare me to death."

"Well, if that happens, I'll make sure to give you mouth to mouth resuscitation."

There was that wicked smile again. Briana had been trying her best to not be so easy, but Charles was making it hard for her. However, she had to hold her ground. If she didn't, then any man could sweet talk his way into her bed. Somehow, she knew this man was totally different. After everything that had happened to her, no guy who's just trying to get in her bed would've stuck around and helped her get herself together. She knew everything about Charles was sincere. At the thought of his sincerity, she felt refreshed. She could let go with this man. He was the one for her.

"So, Ms. Finnegan," Charles said. "Has a good ring to it, don't you think?"

Briana blushed. "I do," she said.

A man on a motorcycle rode through the parking lot followed by three other motorists. Briana watched as they did tricks on their bikes. Slowly, a crowd started to form.

"Are you interested in riding?" Charles asked.

"Definitely," Briana said. "I would love the rush and freedom I'm sure it gives."

"Maybe you rode in your past life," Charles said.

Briana turned from the show to Charles. "That would be really nice. Can you see me?" She got on her knees in a rider's position and bounced lifting her arms in the air as if she were holding on to the handles. "Vroom Vroom!" she said.

Charles laughed. "That's the sexiest thing I've ever seen," he said. Briana fell to the side with laughter. "You might just be a natural. We should take some classes."

"Really?" Briana's eyes lit up. "That would be fantastic. Don't chicken out on me at the last minute, now."

Charles raised an eyebrow. "You're joking, right?"

"If you're scared, just say you are, and I might let you back out of it," Briana teased, but couldn't hold her laughter. She fell over in a fit of giggles.

Charles pulled her into his lap. "Oh, you got jokes, huh? It's okay, I can show you better than I can tell you," he said.

As their laughter subsided, Briana reached down for his plate and fork fed him a mouth full of chicken pot pie.

"Mmmm, still warm and everything. How did you manage to do that?"

"I've got the magic touch."

"Yes, you do," Charles said. His voice sent tremors through her earlobe as his mouth touched it slightly. He trailed his tongue around it and placed soft kisses on the back of her neck. "I can't seem to keep my hands off you," he said with passion and intensity spilling from his lips.

"I don't seem to mind, either," Briana responded.

"Where have you been all my life?" he asked.

"That's a good question." She took another forkful of chicken pot pie and fed it to him.

Watching him gave her butterflies. Oh, who was she kidding? There was nothing this man could do that would turn her off. She turned around in his lap full circle to face him.

"I don't think that's such a good idea," he said and she poked her lip out. "You're so sexy when you pout."

"Don't make me move, I'm comfortable like this. Besides,

I like to watch you eat." Briana put another forkful of chicken pot pie into his mouth. "I can't very well send you back to the firehouse with an empty stomach, now can I?"

"After spending time with you, I'd have had my fill. Trust me."

Charles leaned in and took the next forkful into his mouth, keeping his eyes on Briana. She trailed the tip of her tongue across the bottom of her top lip, their eyes still connected, and fed him the rest of his plate.

"My turn," he said as he picked up her plate and fed her.

# Chapter Six

Tiana slid out of bed and stood in front of the window. The view from Chris' loft was amazing. She turned and looked back at him. He slept soundly and his face looked peaceful. Truth was, Tiana should've been sleeping too. The sex they'd just shared was more than enough to have someone knocked out for the night, but her mind couldn't help but roam.

Chris had been blowing up her phone, trying to get her attention, but she'd been so preoccupied with becoming Briana that she'd kind of neglected him. He'd given her an ultimatum and she caved. Chris was the type of guy good girls went for, which is probably the reason why Tiana had been avoiding him. Nevertheless, having him as her sidepiece was enjoyable in more ways than one.

For starters, she was able to be herself around him. He called her Tiana and she enjoyed it tremendously. When they went out, he wined and dined her only at the best restaurants. Chris was a total gentleman, opening doors for her, and treating her like a princess. He'd even slid his Capital One Visa card in her purse while she went to the restroom without telling her. When she forgot to pay her cell phone bill, she went in her purse for her Visa and noticed the card.

"What is this?" she'd questioned him.

"What does it look like?" he responded.

"Okay, captain obvious, I know what it is. The question is, why is it in my purse?"

He chuckled. "Because I want you to have it. I want to make our relationship official, and I don't want you to want for anything. The only way I can be sure of that is if you take my card."

"Then what will you use?"

"I've got another one," he said. "Capital One didn't stop at that one when they made it."

"Real funny," she said as a small grin flashed across her face.

Tiana really couldn't ask for a better man, so why is it that she couldn't stop thinking about Justin? Was it all in her mind? Of course, he thought she was Briana, but when he looked in her eyes she could swear he saw her, and that made Tiana want him even more. She'd made up her mind that she wouldn't give either one of them up. She couldn't, not now, anyway. Her life was good and it was going to stay that way no matter what she had to do.

If Briana had died, Tiana would probably be sleeping like a champ right now. No worries in the world, two men who loved her dearly, a little family, a career in photography, what more could a girl ask for? But no, she had to live. Tiana shook her head. She still couldn't believe it. As bad as that car accident was, there was no way on this earth she should've survived. Tiana was convinced the Gods were against her.

She shook her head again. What was she thinking? The Gods were against her? Who said there was a God? She was always skeptical, but the way things seemed to be working in Briana's favor, she wasn't too sure she should be. She breathed a heavy sigh and rotated her shoulders. Justin thought she was having a girl's night out with some friends from her photography studio, so he wouldn't expect her in until three a.m. He told her to make sure this was the last time she went out for a while, so she had to make the most of it.

Tiana looked at the clock on the wall above the television. It was two thirty. She glanced back at Chris. He would not take it too well if she left in the middle of the night again. He was over and done with that. Tiana let her mind wander for another ten minutes before tip toeing over to her Michael Kors handbag. Reaching in, she retrieved her cell phone and checked for missed calls or text messages. She had two texts. They were both from Justin.

***Hey bae, hope you're having a good time tonight. I'm missing you.***

The last one read, "***If I'm sleep when you get home wake me up, I don't want to miss a moment that I can have you in my arms.***"

Tiana's head fell into her hand. She was about to text him some bogus made up lie about being too drunk and spending the night over one of her girlfriend's house because she couldn't drive home, but the way Justin was texting made her want to go to him. *He really does love me,* she thought. Every time she thought about it a part of her would deny it. *He doesn't love you,* it would taunt. *He loves his wife, his true woman, you're an imposter.* She hated the thoughts. It was the one thing that made her keep Chris on the side. Even if that was true, he was enjoying and falling in love with Tiana because technically she wasn't Briana. That's the lie she told herself over and over.

After that last thought, she sent him a text. ***Hey, man of my dreams, I seem to have had a little too much to drink. I'm going to take a nap over Chelsea's to wear off some of this alcohol. I love you, see you bright and early.***

Tiana sent the message, checked to make sure her phone was still on silent, then dropped it into her handbag. She turned and went back to the window to ponder whether that was the right call. The last thing she wanted Justin to think was that she was cheating on him, which she was, but he was gullible enough to believe her lies. He believed everything she'd told him thus far, so as long as that was the case, she wouldn't worry about it.

She went and stood in front of Chris' California king bed. His caramel complexion glistened in the moonlight. Still, he slept softly. Tiana envied him for it. His mind was so at ease; he could sleep like a baby. She crawled into bed and removed the silver silk sheets from his waist and mounted him. She trailed kisses up his chest to his neck, giving it a little suck.

He stirred, his head turned and he came face to face with her. He gave her a devious smile and checked the time. "You're still here," he said. His voice was deep and heavy.

"Yes, I am, what are you going to do about it?" she asked.

He rolled her over and placed himself between her thighs. "Girl, I'm going to have to tame you," Chris said.

"And how do you suppose you'll do that?"

"I've got my ways."

"I think I may like that," she responded.

"I know you will."

He kissed her softly on her forehead, leading a trail down her face to her lips. As they were getting into the throes of romance, there was a knock at the door. Not just any knock, a fierce knock. Whoever was on the outside wanted to get in badly.

Simultaneously, Chris and Tiana's heads flew toward the staircase.

"Who is knocking on your door at this time of night?" Tiana questioned, sitting up and folding her arms.

"Probably my son's mother. She's the only one with the nerve."

Tiana stood up and grabbed her house robe. "I'll take care of this," she said.

"No, baby, hold up. I've got it. The last thing I want is for you two to go at it."

"I don't plan on going at it with her, I'm simply going to tell her to stop knocking on our door."

"Our door?" he questioned. "Does that mean you've taken into consideration me asking you to move in?"

"Maybe?" she lied.

Tiana was digging herself into a big hole. There was no way she would be able to do that and she knew it, but it pacified him for the time being.

"When you're sure," he said, "let me know, and I will get you a key and you can start answering the door. But take my word for it, talking to her now at this hour is not a good idea. She's probably drunk, been out with her ratchet friends, and now wants to throw a fit about nothing. I seem to be target practice for her since she blames me for us not being together anymore."

The knocks continued, and now the woman was screaming his name at the front door. Chris rounded the stairs that led to the first level of his loft and looked out of the peep hole. Sure enough, it was his son's mother and she looked lit up. He took a deep breath and opened the door.

She stumbled as the door swung open.

"Why are you knocking on my door at three o'clock in the morning?"

"Because I need to t-talk," she stuttered, "to you!"

"No, Sandra, you need to go home. Where is Christopher?" he asked.

"Well, he ain't gone be at the club with me!" she stated matter-of-factly. "So that was a dumb question."

Chris sighed, unable to continue the dance they did at his front door. "Go home," he said, and slammed the door in her face.

"Oh no you didn't!" he heard her say from the other side of the door.

Boom! Boom! Boom! She beat on the door again and crossed her arms. "I'm not leaving until you talk to me, so you might as well come back to the door. I don't care if your neighbors call the police. I will stand here until they arrive!"

Tiana pushed past Chris. He reached out and grabbed her arm to stop her.

"Look, this heffa ain't going away, and I'm about to give her a piece of my mind. She's ruining our night!"

"Baby, calm down, I got this."

Tiana huffed. "I can't tell!"

She pivoted on her heels and went to the kitchen. The banging on the door continued. She shook her head and ran her fingers through her hair. Looking in the cupboard she removed a wine glass and popped the cork on a bottle of Emmolo Merlot that had been sitting on ice since their earlier tryst. She rolled her eyes as she listened to Chris in the front room arguing with his son's mother. This is the last thing she needed. She sipped from the glass and closed her eyes as the caramelized plum, brown spices and rich fruit flavor oozed down her throat. She took another swig; it was delicious, but what would've been better is if she could get back into bed with Chris.

"Enough of this," she said.

Tiana made her way back to the living room where the couple was still arguing. She cleared her throat and stepped into view, letting her robe open just enough to show off her bare chest and panties. She took another swig of her wine as she watched a look of fury cross the woman's face. Tiana almost laughed. Chris didn't look amused, but he wouldn't dare tell her otherwise.

"Baby, should I go? I don't want to cause any trouble," Tiana purred innocently.

Chris gave her a knowing look. He knew that she was aware that their argument had nothing to do with her. Tiana just wanted to make her presence known.

"No, sweetheart, go back to bed. I'll be there in a second," he said to appease her. The last thing he wanted to do was argue with Tiana. No sooner than the words had left his mouth, another woman rounded the corner.

"Sandra, let's go. What are you doing, girl?"

"She's up here making an ass of herself," Chris said. Sandra looked back at Tiana and scowled. "I was trying to have a conversation with my baby daddy, but I guess he too busy entertaining thots," she said.

That was all Tiana could handle. She flew across the room and tossed the rest of the Merlot into Sandra's face and slapped her with the other hand before Chris could pull her away. The women yelled and bickered at each other before Tiana broke away and stomped upstairs. Sandra, Chris and Sandra's friend were yelling now, going back and forth about police and restraining orders.

When Tiana returned downstairs, she was fully dressed, keys in hand. Three pairs of eyes looked her way as she sauntered past Chris.

"Tiana! Don't leave like this."

"Whatever," Tiana said.

Chris went after her.

"You're so disrespectful," he heard Sandra saying as he flew around her. "Here I am, trying to talk to you, and you run after her?"

"Tiana!" Chris yelled, ignoring Sandra.

Tiana stopped at the elevators and pressed the down button three times.

"Please don't leave like this, baby," Chris said.

"You know what? This is the last thing I have time to deal with. And you want me to move in with you, but you can't handle your baby's mom." She tisked. "No," she said, putting her hand in his face. "I don't have to deal with it and I won't. And I hate the word, thot, it's a childish word used to degrade women, and I won't tolerate anyone speaking to me like that."

"Baby, I can guarantee you this almost never happens."

"Unhuh, but you knew it was her at the door before you even answered it. Tells me it's happened more times than not."

"It's happened two other times since we've broken up. She's just scorned because she feels like I left her for you."

"She doesn't even know me."

"She knows of you, though."

Tiana gave him a skeptical glance.

"When I first met you, I had friendships with about five other women. I've told them all about you because I'm serious about you, including Sandra."

Tiana gave him a sincere look. This man was really good for her. She would surely ruin him. If he knew what her life was like now, and what she was up to, he wouldn't want anything to do with her.

"Baby, please don't go."

Chris reached for Tiana and pulled her into his arms. He brought his caramel lips to hers and tasted the Merlot on her tongue.

"You sure do know how to make a woman change her mind," she said.

A smile lightened his face. There she stood in the hallway in front of the elevators with this handsome man with no shirt on. Sandra and her friend rounded the corner. Sandra grabbed

Chris's shoulder and yanked him off of Tiana. Neither of them expected it.

Tiana reached into her purse, pulled out a pink and white three eighty handgun, and pointed it at Sandra. Chris, Sandra, and her friend all stepped back.

"I don't want any trouble. This has nothing to do with me," her friend said.

Tiana swallowed, her eyes turned in to small slits. "If I were you, Sandra," she said, her voice frank and deadly, "I would let go of my man, and hightail it out of here."

"Baby…" Chris started.

"Un huh, you had your chance to handle this situation. Now it's my turn." Tiana turned back to Sandra. "Bye, and if I ever see you around this loft again, I won't hesitate to blow your head off your shoulders."

Sandra's friend grabbed her hand and they flew past Tiana to the stairwell, forgetting about the open elevator door.

Tiana tucked her gun back into her purse and straightened her shoulders. "Shall we?" she said, motioning for them to return to his loft.

He smirked. "So, you Billie Badass, now?"

"I can be," she admitted.

He didn't know how close to the truth that really was.

# *Chapter Seven*

## *Adler and Adams Associates LLC*

Justin stepped into his office, removed his suit jacket and tossed it over the back of his chair. He'd just won the case against the multimillion corporation, Sedway, who had a class action law suit brought against them by their employees. Sedway had been accused of firing African-American employees once they reached a certain pay grade, in an attempt to make sure the company's highest paid employees were Caucasian Americans.

Justin walked to his desk and sat down in his leather high back swivel chair. He loosened his tie, rolled his sleeves up to his elbows, and rubbed the back of his neck, then stretched his fingers and powered on his MacBook Pro. After entering his password, he pondered on the plans he had for tonight.

Steven McNair stuck his head in the door and lightly tapped. Justin looked up. "Congratulations on the win, man, you are a boss!" he said.

Justin gave him a lazy smile. "Thanks, it's all in a day's work," he said.

"Now that's bull," Steve said. "Sedway had six high powered attorneys who were cocky and sure they were going to win the suit. The look on their faces when the judge handed over the victory to Adler, Adams & Associates was priceless!"

Justin's smile never wavered. He sat back and propped his leg up on his thigh, intertwining his fingers.

"Just admit it, man, you are the boss! Can't nobody mess with you, that's why you've made partner and are one of the highest paid attorneys in this region!"

Justin lifted an eyebrow. "How do you know I'm one of the highest paid attorneys?"

"Come on, man, everybody knows. You made the cover of Top Attorney magazine! Anybody who didn't know you then, knows you now."

Justin was tickled. Of course, the magazine had catapulted him into super lawyer status, but he was only dealing the hand that God had dealt him, which was a good one.

"I swear, if Briana had stayed, you guys would have been the highest paid power couple. You don't even need this law firm. You could have one with your name on it. Many attorneys would line up to work for you, and there would be no shortage of employees. Imagine this, it would read Gable Attorneys at Law, LLC."

"Would you come work for me?" Justin asked.

"In a heartbeat! You offering me a job?"

Justin laughed. "When I do decide to go there, you will be my first hire."

"That would be such an honor!" Steve said.

Steve McNair was one of Adams and Adler's interns. He was sharp, very smart, and a quick study. In no time, Justin would have him winning high profile cases.

"Good!" Justin said.

"Some of the guys are going out for a celebration, they sent me in here to make sure you're coming."

"And here I thought you wanted to congratulate me," Justin said.

Afraid that his presence was taken the wrong way, Steve stumbled to reply. "Oh, of course. I um didn't mean to make it seem like—"

"It's okay, I'm just messing with you, kid," Justin said. "Tell the boys I won't be able to make it tonight." At the question on Steve's face, Justin went on to say, "I've got plans."

"Are you sure?" Steve said.

"Yeah, but I'll take a raincheck."

"Okay," Steve said.

He waltzed out the room and Justin turned his attention back to his MacBook Pro. On Google, he searched prices for flights to Barbados. This was going to be the trip of a lifetime. Justin was pulling out all the stops for his wife. She would never want to leave the island. He thought about their family and how the Lord had blessed them in a mighty way.

Their life had changed dramatically. After Justin had finished law school, it was Briana's turn. She graduated earlier than he did and he was proud of her, but the reality was the romance had left them. They were so busy working and taking care of the kids that they'd left no time for them. It had gone on so long, Justin didn't think they'd ever be able to get it back. If one was coming in the door, the other was going out. Their love life had become non-existent.

Justin was convinced that the state of their marriage is what had caused her to make such a drastic career change, but so far, Brian hadn't admitted it. He wondered why. Sure, she'd told him photography was her first love, but he didn't believe it. He remembered the nights she spoke about cases with such vigor and excitement that she could hardly wait to get back to work. That can't be falsified. Now their romance had picked up and gone full steam ahead. Sure, his teenage daughter was going through some adolescent issues, but what teenager didn't? For the most part life, was good.

Justin had plans to take his wife out to celebrate; he was a family man. Even though he had enough money and power now to have practically whatever he wanted, he was raised on humble beginnings. And being a man of integrity, he would stay that way, which made him one of kind. Although things had turned out great with her career change, he wished she still worked with him at the firm.

Steven was right, they could be a power couple and completely take over the region, but he would support his wife in whatever endeavors she embarked on. It was strange to him that she'd decided to go with photography, with that being Tiana's career choice. Justin had never really been around Tiana. It was a shame because she was his sister in law, but he had no idea what kind of person she was. The only thing he knew about her was what Briana had told him and that she was identical to her, fiercely so.

When Briana had waltzed in the house at seven o'clock Sunday morning, it had taken him by surprise. Briana was never the type of person to stay out so late, but because she'd promised never to do it again, Justin had dropped the issue. After making sure she was okay, he'd asked her if she wanted him and the girls to wait for her and they would go to the late service, but she'd refused.

"You guys are already ready, and I don't want to make you wait. I'll pull the service up on my computer and watch it online," she'd said.

"Are you sure, baby? It wouldn't be a problem," he'd offered.

She'd insisted on them going without her, so they did. It was kind of weird, but he shrugged it off, and even though deep down his gut was turning about her not coming home Saturday night, he trusted his wife. There was no reason for him not to. So he, Taylor and Denise got in his Escalade and went to church.

When Justin arrived back home, the house was empty. He phoned her, but got no answer. He gave her a minute then called her back. She answered, saying that she was out getting something for dinner. *Of course she was,* Justin thought. *What else would she be doing?*

Now, he wanted to reward her for always being by his side, for allowing him to have her hand in marriage, for bearing him two beautiful children, for being a housewife while he got his degree. She had put her education on hold to let him finish, and of course, when he was done, he'd returned the favor. He wanted to reward her for being the love of his life, he wanted to reward her for everything. She was all he could want and more, and he felt guilty at times for wondering if their marriage would make it. Just because they'd lost their way at one point didn't mean they couldn't get it back, right?

How many men could be so lucky? Not many, although Justin knew it had nothing to do with luck. They were simply blessed. He picked up the phone and dialed his travel agent. The phone rang twice before his agent answered the phone.

"Hey, Trevor, how are you?" Justin asked.

"It's a great day, and I'm doing just fine. How about yourself, Mr. Gable?"

"Everything is good on my end. I'm looking to travel internationally to Barbados within the next three weeks. Do you think you can whip me up a good flight, or would it be more beneficial to take a cruise to the island?" he asked.

"It depends on what you would like, sir. I can definitely get you some tickets, but if you're looking to take a cruise before getting to the island, we can do that too. I can find you a great deal on a cruise. How many days are you looking to stay in Barbados?" Trevor asked.

"I'm thinking a seven day, six-night trip."

"Are you wanting to spend the full time on the island or are you willing to split that time up with the cruise?" Trevor asked.

"That's a good question," Justin said. "Let's split the time up on a cruise."

"Okay, now, Mr. Gable, are your passports still valid?"

"Of course," Justin said.

"Once I find a trip, I'll call you back with the information to get your final approval. At that time, if there are any changes you want to make, please let me know then because once the payment is made the trip is non-refundable."

"You've told me that before, Trevor," Justin said a chuckle in his voice.

"I know. I just have to tell you again."

"That's fine, Trevor, I'll add the travel insurance as usual and ask the wife if she wants to take a cruise over there or a straight flight. So until I hear back from you, check prices for both, if you don't mind."

"I don't mind at all," Trevor said.

"Good, I'll wait to hear from you then."

"Talk to you soon, Mr. Gable. Have a good day."

Justin disconnected the call. He sat back and relaxed his shoulder, letting his head fall back on his chair. Tonight, he'd made plans to go to STK, a Midtown Atlanta restaurant known for its chic décor and upscale cuisine.

Justin checked his Rolex and stood from his chair. He grabbed his suit jacket and picked up his briefcase before making his way out of his office. Out in the hallway, he grabbed the elevator with Jackie Donahue, the front desk secretary. She was dressed in a ruffle top crème colored blouse, a pin stripe skirt that went down to her knees, crème pantyhose, and two inch heels. Her light brown hair lay straight past her shoulders, stopping in the middle of her back.

Her light brown eyes turned and assessed him. Just about all the men in the law firm had a thing or two to say about Jackie. All good, of course. She was easy on the eyes.

Her peachy lips turned into a beautiful smile. "I'm surprised you're still here," she said. "Congratulations on your win."

Her smile brightened and she tossed her hair back, giving Justin the perfect glimpse of her chest. The two buttons at the top were loose, showing a nice amount of cleavage.

He knew a flirt when he saw one. "Yeah, just finished talking to the travel agent about a trip to Barbados for me and the missus," he said.

Her eyes grew wide in surprise. "I am so jealous," she said.

"I'm sure your husband would do the same for you," Justin said, knowing very well that Jackie was as single as they come.

"If only I could be so lucky!" she said. They got off the elevator at the ground floor. "Well, I guess I'll head to the bar with the rest of the staff. Why is everyone out celebrating your victory except for you?"

"A victory for me is a victory for the firm," he said. "Besides, I'm celebrating, just in another way."

Jackie whistled. "Lucky girl."

Justin winked and walked to his Escalade. He pulled out of the garage and got on the highway headed to his home. On the way, he dialed his wife, letting the Bluetooth connect to his truck so he could talk hands-free.

"Hello," she said.

"What are you wearing?"

Tiana giggled. "What should I be wearing?" she purred.

In that instant, she'd almost made him change his mind,

cancel the plans, and go straight to his home, but he held out. "Put on something, I'm taking you out to celebrate."

"Really?" she sounded intrigued. "What are we celebrating?"

Justin's brow furrowed. His wife always kept up with his cases. After all, it was their thing. One of the connections they had. "Remember my trial today?" When Tiana didn't respond, he said, "The same one I've been handling for months now."

No response.

Justin was appalled.

"I'm so sorry, honey. I've been so busy with the photography studio I haven't really noticed. Will you forgive me?"

"Haven't noticed?" he questioned.

"I'm sorry, I really am, I'll make it up to you."

Justin was disappointed. Every time his wife did something unusual he would question her and she would put his worries to rest, but this was unexplainable by far.

"First time for everything, right?" Tiana said, trying to bring some innocence into the conversation.

"Who are you, and what have you done with my wife?" he said.

Alarmed, Tiana stuttered, "Wha-what do you mean?" She placed her hand to her chest to calm her racing heart.

"What I mean is, Briana Alexis Gable would never forget to at least check in on my cases. I realize you've changed professions, but what about all of the nights you've asked me how my case was going? Did you forget about those?" he asked. "I'm pulling up," he said and disconnected the call.

On the other end of the line, Tiana cursed something unintelligible. How could she forget to check up on his cases? She had to make things better, and asap. She ran into the closet and went through some of Briana's clothes. Since she'd taken over, she'd been wearing her wardrobe, not wanting to change everything too drastically, but some of her sister's clothes were just too conservative. She was ideal when it came to the saying, a lady in the street and a freak in the bed.

Tiana shook her head, trying to erase that last thought.

"Ah ha!" she said, coming across a sexy red number that hung off the shoulders and stopped right at the knees.

She shimmied into the dress and ran into the master bathroom. In the mirror, she spruced up her hair. The layered cut looked great, and it bounced right off her shoulders. She checked her teeth and decided to give them an extra brush. After applying some light makeup, she decided to do something different and add eye makeup. Dramatic as it was, it was still hot.

Tiana splashed herself with Chanel perfume before sliding into Briana's red five inch heels. Fortunately for her, Justin liked to shower Briana, and the Manolo Blahniks were welcome gift for the hell she had to endure every day, pretending to be Briana. She grabbed her red and black clutch and her cell phone that was buzzing in the middle of the bed.

It was Chris.

Tiana sighed. He was trying to require all of her time, and as much as she loved being showered by two men, trying to keep on top of things was a bit much. However, she would do what she had to do because she wasn't ready to give up either of them. Tiana reasoned if she ever had to, she would choose Justin. Why leave a life of luxury for love? Besides, she loved Justin, and he loved her, or so she told herself.

She sent Chris a quick text. ***Sorry, love, at a late night photoshoot for a musical artist. Will get back with you soon. Kiss.***

Before shutting the phone off, she did a quick Google search to see what Justin's case was about. Of course it would be all over the internet and news. He was a high powered attorney. She went down the stairs. The girls were at their granny's, so she didn't have to worry about talking to Taylor about watching her little sister.

Justin exited the car and rounded to the passenger side to open the door. "You look beautiful," he said.

"Thank you, honey. You always look debonair."

He gave her a small smile. She could tell he was feeling a bit upset about the fact that she was completely lost when it came to his case. Lucky for her, she'd done five minutes of research on Google about the case, so over dinner she would casually say something about it and pretend like her not paying attention was all a joke. At least she would try; it had to work.

There was an awkward silence in the car. Tiana didn't know how to start the conversation. "So, congratulations are in order, even though I always knew you would win," she said, giving him a demure smile.

"Did you, now?" he said his voice tight.

"You haven't lost a case since… since… since I don't know when!" She laughed nervously. "That's how long it's been. You never lose a case. You're brilliant."

She could see him relax a little. "I'm glad you think so."

"I always have, haven't I?"

He dipped his head in silent agreement. Even though she was trying to lighten the mood, tension was obviously still in the air.

"I made dinner tonight," she said.

"What did you make?"

"I baked some pork chops, homemade mac and cheese, green beans, dinner rolls and steamed carrots." She smiled at him.

"Thank you for making dinner. I didn't mean to make it go to waste, I just thought tonight was a night worth celebrating. We'll eat it as leftovers tomorrow, how's that?"

"That's fine. I'm not mad at all. Whatever you want, honey."

Justin gave her a once over. "Whatever I want?"

"Yeah, did I say something wrong?"

"Just interesting."

Tiana wondered what that meant, but she didn't want to go into it. She was starting to feel like she should just close her mouth. Even with the slight conversation, the tension in the car was still thick.

"So, I'm guessing Sedway and their multiple attorneys were pretty upset when the judge handed down the verdict."

Justin peered at Tiana. "I thought you didn't remember anything about the case."

Tiana shrugged. "So, maybe I remember some things." She gave him a modest smile.

Justin grinned. "Woman, don't play with me like that."

Tiana laughed, wanting to wipe the invisible sweat off her brow. "Like I said before, I always knew you could do it."

"You know what would've made it better?" he said.

"What's that?" she asked.

"If you were right there in the courtroom with me."

At the horrified look on Tiana's face, Justin said, "Let me ask you a question, and you know you can be honest with me. I won't feel one way or the other with how you answer. Inquiring minds just want to know."

Tiana fidgeted in her seat, feeling uncomfortable with how this may go. "Okay," she said.

"Did you go to law school just to impress me, or did you seriously have a love for the law?"

Tiana exhaled the breath she was holding. "I really loved it in the beginning, but I think I outgrew it." Justin didn't look convinced. "Does it bother you that I don't practice anymore?"

"I wouldn't say it bothered me, more so that I feel a little empty without you on my team."

"Well, honey, I'm still on your team, just not in the office."

"That's what I meant."

They pulled up in front of STK. A valet attendant walked to the driver side door as Justin opened it. "Would you like valet, sir?"

"Of course," he said.

They exchanged places as Justin made his way around to Tiana. He opened her door and she stepped out.

"Beautiful," Justin said looking at her like he'd never seen her before.

"You already said that back at the house, Tiana said.

"And I'm saying it again." He took her hand and pulled her away from the curb then entwined their arms, and they stepped in stride, making their way into the restaurant.

The host greeted them and asked for their names. "Gable."

The host ran his eyes over the reservations. "Your table is ready. Jasmine here will escort you," he said.

Justin dipped his head as they followed the man named Jasmine, whose strut clearly held a feminine touch. At their table, Jasmine gave them two menus.

"Would you like anything to drink?"

"I'll have your peach tea," Tiana said.

"Water for me."

"Very well, your waiter will be Alice tonight. Have a look over the menus and she will be right with you."

"Thank you."

"Food smells good in here," Tiana said. "I'm betting they have excellent chefs."

"Says the woman who acts as if she's never ate here before."

"It's been a while."

Tiana hoped that was true. She thought she knew everything about Briana, the longer she tried to live her life, the more she realized how much she didn't. Even though their looks were identical, right down to the freckles under their eyes, their love and taste for life itself was completely different. Six months of pretending to be Briana had opened Tiana's eyes a lot about how different her sister really was. If only they didn't look so much alike. It was so annoying to Tiana, and bothered her to no end.

"I think I'll have the Roasted Rack of Lamb," Justin said interrupting Tiana's thoughts. "What would you like, sweetheart?"

"I'm thinking the Scottish Salmon," she answered.

The waiter returned to the table and took their orders. Over dinner, they talked and had casual conversation before getting into the case. Tiana listened attentively to the details. She wouldn't be caught off her game again. She'd made sure if he gave her a pop quiz later, she'd ace it. After they ate, the waiter came back to take their desert orders.

"Bae, let's share a dessert," Tiana said.

"Sure, what would you like?"

"I'm thinking—"

"Wait, let me guess," Justin interrupted her. "The Almond Fudge Brownie."

Tiana smiled and clapped her hands softly. "How'd you know?"

"I pay attention."

Tiana wondered if that was a dig at her, or if he was being sincere. Either way, she didn't let her smile falter.

"Very well," the waiter said. He refilled their drinks and left the table to get their desert.

Tiana reached across the table and grabbed Justin's hand. "I love you," she said.

"I love you too," he responded, bringing her hand to his lips for a kiss.

Tiana was so into him. She could love Justin forever. This

could be her life. Nothing would ever have to change, she had to make sure of it. She made up her mind right then to do away with her sister. What was she waiting for anyway?

"Tiana?"

Her body tensed at the sound of his voice. Letting go of Justin's hand, she looked around to see who had called her and came face to face with her lover, Chris, as his stride brought him to the table. She had to bite down on her tongue to keep from calling out his name.

Recovering quickly, she smiled and held out her hand to greet him. "Briana," was all she said.

"Excuse me?" Chris said, his face a mask of anger.

*He is sexy, even when he is pissed off,* she thought.

"This is my husband, Justin," Tiana said, introducing Justin before things got out of hand.

"What is going on?" Chris asked.

Tiana lost her voice as Justin snickered. "Allow me to explain. This is Briana, Tiana's identical twin."

Justin and Tiana watched the emotions on Chris's face go from angered to confusion. Tiana could see the tightness in his shoulders relax slightly.

"It's okay, it happens all the time," Justin said. "Imagine my reaction the first time it happened before I knew Briana was a twin. I thought she was trying to play me." Justin laughed. "That must be what you're feeling right now."

Chris took a step back and looked from Justin to Tiana. "Is this some kind of joke?" he said.

"I assure you it isn't." Justin confirmed.

"Why hasn't she ever mentioned you before?" Chris asked, studying every intricate detail of Tiana's face.

"That doesn't surprise me. It's not something she typically brings up, unless of course, she's serious about you. And by that, I mean marriage," Tiana said with a small chuckle.

"Fascinating," Chris murmured, looking from Tiana to Justin.

He held his hand out. "I'm Chris Fredrickson, by the way. When I saw your wife from across the room, I figured you must be the reason she's not answering her phone."

Tiana's gut tightened, and again, she lost her voice.

Justin laughed. "It's no problem at all. Like I said, it's happened more times than not. Maybe one day, whenever Briana speaks to her sister, she can talk her into double dating."

Tiana's stomach was getting tighter and tighter.

"I would love that," Chris said, taking his business card out and sliding it to Justin. "Here's my card, if you ever need your canvas painted, I'd love to do it for you." As he said this, his eyes were back on Tiana.

The smile of appreciation and confidence on her face didn't match the mortification she felt on the inside. But she kept her cool. Tiana reached for the business card at the same time that Justin did.

"That won't be necessary," she said, finding her voice once more.

Chris frowned and gave her another questioning look.

"Why not?" both the men said in unison.

"Because Tiana is a photographer, she may feel some kind of way about us using someone else's services."

"This is art, honey. A canvas and a photo are not the same."

"I know, I'm just saying."

Justin pulled the card to him and placed it in the inside of his breast pocket. "I don't think she'll mind," he said and winked.

Tiana turned her head slightly to the left, enough for the tattoo on the back of her neck to reveal itself.

It caught Chris's eye. "You even have the same tattoo?" He reached out to touch her neck.

"Please do not touch my wife, I'll have to charge you for that."

Chris and Tiana looked at Justin in shock. Tiana didn't know he had it in him. That was the first time she'd heard Justin be a little spicy.

Justin smiled. "And trust me, you can't afford the tab."

It downright turned Tiana on.

"My bad," Chris said, "no disrespect."

"None taken," Justin said.

"I guess I'll let you guys get back to your meals, sorry for the interruption. If you see Tiana before I do, tell her she's got some explaining to do," Chris said and retreated from their table.

"That never gets old," Justin said.

Tiana couldn't even think straight. What was she going to do about Chris? This was the first time she was happy she had a twin, because under normal circumstances, she would have never gotten away with this. And in her gut, she wasn't all too sure that she had.

# Chapter Eight

"Can you grab two or three of those fresh tomatoes?" Charles asked Briana. "Make sure they're fresh, too."

Briana bent over and surveyed the tomatoes. She picked three of them up and put them in a plastic bag. "Let me get this straight, you're going to cook lasagna and use your homemade sauce?"

"Yes ma'am, and you're going to love it."

"A man that can cook. I've been loving that and taking advantage for it three weeks now. I can't believe it's been that long since I've been out of the hospital."

"Time flies when you're having fun."

"Who said I was having fun?"

Charles gave her a crooked grin. "I assumed you were. Am I boring you to death already?"

"Not at all, I'm just messing with you."

They strolled the grocery store picking up other fresh items for dinner. Briana couldn't be happier in her circumstance. Charles literally took care of everything she needed. Whenever she got depressed about her past, he would cheer her right up with talks about her future. Briana imagined a future with him. Maybe it was too soon for that, but Charles was all she knew, and she couldn't see why she would need anyone else. Especially with the passionate way he looked at her and the heated way he spoke to her.

Charles was feeling the same way. Since his wife and children died in that horrific car accident, he hadn't entertained the thought of being with someone else, but having Briana around was a welcome change. It was nice to be able to open up about everything he'd been holding in without judgment, and their sexual attraction to each other was overwhelming.

"Let's get some extra items for the week since we're here," Charles said.

Briana picked up a bag of frozen vegetables. "Are there some peas over there?"

He stepped around the basket and went for the bag of peas, standing so close to Briana she could feel his energy. Anytime he got near her she wanted him to stay, but she would never say it. Like he was reading her mind, Charles faced her. He couldn't resist. With his free arm, he brought Briana closer to him and kissed her. It sent butterflies through Briana's chest and her body woke up with want and need. They kissed for the better part of a minute, enjoying the taste of each other's lips.

Charles kept his eyes open while kissing her. Briana's lips were sweet and he wanted to watch her reaction. Briana was in la la land. Her eyes were closed and she melted where she stood. When he pulled away from her, it was slow and sensual. Briana stood still in his embrace, her face flushed.

"I'm not sorry," he said.

"Me either," she responded.

A smile spread across Charles' face. He took her by the hand and they walked like two people in love. After they picked out the rest of their food, they headed to the register.

Standing behind a magazine rack, Tiana watched their

every move. It didn't take her sister long to find a new love. *Too bad it won't last,* Tiana thought. Briana being alive posed a big threat to Tiana, and she couldn't take the chance of letting her mess things up. Tiana watched them complete their purchase then she did an about face and tossed the magazine she pretended to read.

Running into Chris at the restaurant had her completely disturbed. She laughed at the thought of her and Briana on a double date. "Never," she said through gritted teeth.

After leaving the restaurant, Justin could tell she was bothered. He'd questioned her mood all the way home, asking everything from if she was upset about the way he came off to Chris, or if there was something she wasn't telling him. When they got home, she reassured him there was nothing to be concerned about. She played it off as if she was just hurt that her sister wouldn't tell someone she was a twin, as much as they ran into people who knew one or the other. If there was an award for best actress in a real life drama, she would definitely get.

Justin had consoled her and held her all night, whispering sweet promises in her ear. Things that Tiana knew could not be possible. Promises about her and Briana finding their way to each other and growing close once again. It was a fairy tale, but only because Tiana didn't want that. She'd rolled her eyes and tried to stay in her role, but she was getting sick of hearing about Briana. No amount of conversation would ever change the way she felt about her. Tiana didn't like to share the spotlight, and that's what brought her to her current situation. Briana had to go.

Tiana sighed. Watching her sister fall in love was so funny. She had no clue that she was cheating on her husband. It made Tiana joyful inside. The poor guy she was with was just as in love, and he was drop dead gorgeous. That was another thing Tiana despised. For her and Briana to be identical, Briana always seemed to end up with the best looking men. Now what was Tiana missing about that?

It made Tiana even more irritable. Although Chris was very sweet on the eyes, he was still no Justin or whoever this new guy was Briana was tagging along with. Once Tiana had got Justin into bed, she'd slithered her way on top of him and made love for hours.

Outside, she got behind the wheel of her Dodge Intrepid and waited like a thief for them to exit. They continued to hold hands, each one carrying a set of bags so their other hand could be free. Tiana rolled her eyes. Briana got on her nerves. Why would God do this to her? Why did she have to have a twin? She would never be able to be her own person until Briana was no longer alive. There was no way around it. It just had to happen.

Charles pulled off in his Audi and whipped around the corner. Tiana tried to follow him without being obvious, and she didn't have to try very hard. Charles and Briana were lost in each other.

Charles turned the radio up as Musiq Soulchild sang about love, and it was perfect timing. When Charles turned the next corner, the Audi swerved and there was a loud POP as the left front wheel tire burst. Surprised, Charles tried to gain control of the wheel, but failed miserably. The Audi ran off the road into a lamppost. The tires spun to a hard stop, kicking up dust. The smell of burnt rubber saturated the air.

Tiana watched them from behind. She could see the air-bags deploy, and she hoped it would tear up Briana's face.

In the Audi, Charles turned to Briana. "Gabrielle, are you okay?" The sting from the airbag had left her with a nose bleed. "Hold on, I got you," Charles said.

Briana moaned. "Aaa, my nose!"

"Tilt your head back, sweetheart," Charles said.

He gently lifted her head and searched his glove compartment for napkins. Briana blinked several times. Dazed and confused, she got a glimpse of a woman's face. The more she blinked, the more the woman's face came into focus. The woman threw her head back and laughed. Her hair was long, past her shoulders, and she wore a green and white workout suit.

*"Briana, you know I'm going to win this time!" The woman took off running, still smiling.*

*"Angela, wait up!" The voice sounded like Briana's.*

The memory faded. The next thing she heard was Charles saying, "The police are on their way."

Briana sat still, trying to figure out what had just happened when it dawned on her. She had just had her first memory.

"Sweetheart, are you okay?" Charles asked.

"I'm not sure," Briana said. "I remember."

Charles froze. "You remember?"

"I remember a woman. Angela."

"Okay, that's a good start. What about her do you remember?" Charles watched her with the same concerned look he wore at the hospital.

"I don't know, I don't know," she repeated.

"That's okay, take your time and think about it."

Briana's head began to spin and her breathing got heavy. Another second went by before she passed out.

"Gabrielle!" Charles yelled, calling her by the name she'd grown used to over the weeks, but she didn't respond. She was already deep off in dream land.

*Behind the wheel of a car, Briana turned into the circle driveway and parked by the front door. Before she could blow her horn, Angela came out dressed in an Anne Taylor business suit that fit her shapely curves with a snug but comfortable hug. Her heels click clacked as she descended the front steps to the car.*

*"Alright, alright now, I see you. Are you trying to out shine me or what?" Briana asked.*

*"Well, it wouldn't take much for me to do that," Angela countered as she got in on the passenger side and shut the door.*

*"Owwww, you got me, but don't hate. You know I look good." Briana snickered.*

*She did look good. Dressed down in a two button Seventh Avenue design studio jacket with a lilac blouse and the signature Seventh Avenue pants to match gave Briana a professional but sexy style. The business suit came from New York and Company, and she was thrilled that it fit her so nicely.*

*"Of course you do, no hate here. I'm just mad you went to New York and Company without me. Now what is that all about?"*

*"Girl, it was a spur of the moment type of thing I didn't mean to leave you out."*

*"How exactly is it spur of the moment when we attend this event every year? You knew it was coming up, so there is no excuse!"*

*"You're right, I know! It's just I hadn't planned to go, I just happened to be in that area and I knew I still didn't have anything to wear to this year's awards luncheon." Briana lowered her voice to an Eartha Kitt growl. "And you know when I go to these events I've gotta be fierce, honey." She snapped her fingers. "Besides, it doesn't look like you needed my shopping expertise. Where'd you get that suit?"*

*"Anne Taylor's official website, they had a sale and I couldn't help myself." The ladies laughed.*

*Briana's phone rang. She looked away from the road for a moment to check her caller ID.*

*"Now you know I'm not with the texting and driving, so put that phone down," Angela said.*

*"Girl, hush, you know I don't text and drive. Besides, that's Justin. I'll call him back when we get parked."*

Angela spoke again, but Briana could no longer make out the words coming from her. In an instant, her eyes snapped open and once again the familiar blur then brightness of hospital lights came into view.

Standing over her, Charles frowned.

"Baby, can you hear me?" he asked.

Briana blinked, feeling heaviness on her head. At any moment she thought she might pass out again.

"Sweetheart," Charles voice came through gentle and worried.

"Justin," Briana said.

Charles paused, watching her intently.

"Justin," Briana said again.

"No, it's Charles," he said.

Briana's vision came into focus. She reached out to caress the side of his face. Her touch soothed him and eased his mind, sending shivers through his body. "Charles," she said.

He smiled. "Yes, love, it's me. We have to stop meeting like this."

She let out a weak chuckle. "What happened?"

"One of the tires on the car popped. The police think the car had been tampered with."

"Who would do such a thing?" Briana asked.

"I wish I could answer that," Charles said. "How do you feel?"

"A little dizzy, but it's getting better."

Charles hesitated then said, "You were dreaming, you were calling out the name Justin. Do you know who that is?"

Briana thought back to her dream. "I'm not sure." She wondered, who Justin could be? A friend, a brother, a lover? The thought made her uneasy. Her pass was becoming more mysterious with this new memory. "I was going to an awards luncheon with Angela."

"Who is Angela? You said her name before passing out when we were still in the car."

"I think she's my best friend," Briana said.

Briana told Charles about her dream. "Then my phone rang and it was Justin. But I never got to find out who he is. I don't remember I just remember his name on my caller ID."

"Are you sure it was a dream, or could it have been a memory?"

"I don't know, maybe—"

They were interrupted by the doctor. "I'm almost certain it was a memory." He walked up to Briana's bedside. "I'm sorry for the intrusion, but you said you were having a memory before you passed out. Nine times out of ten, that's what you were experiencing the whole time."

"But in my first memory I was running alongside Angela. I think we were actually racing. She called me Briana."

"Briana," Charles said. The name sounded like butter coming off his tongue, melting Briana further into her sheets.

"Doesn't matter if the scene changed. When it did, you were still with Angela, so this person must play an important role in your life."

"It's true," she said, looking from the doctor to Charles. "I got the sense that she is a close friend. In my dream, or memory, we were laughing and talking like we'd known each other for years."

"Well, I want to keep a watch over you through the night, if it's alright with you. And you'll be released back into Mr. Finnegan's care in the morning. Is that okay?" The doctor asked.

"Yeah, sure," Briana said.

"Okay, then, get some rest."

The doctor left the room and silence encased them. Briana, hopeful about the chance that her memory would come back.

Charles wondering if she should stay longer. He was going to help her find out who she was.

## *Later That Night...*

"Is everything okay?" Justin asked.

Tiana sat Indian style, biting down on her thumb nail. "Huh?" she said.

Justin sat next to her and scooped her up in his lap. "I asked you what's wrong. You've been pacing most of the night, now you're sitting here in a trance biting all of your finger nails off."

"Oh, nothing's wrong, baby. Just a deadline at work."

Justin frowned. "I thought you were finished with the project."

"I was put on an emergency project and I only have three days to complete it," she lied.

"Well tell them that's too soon and you can't take it, but there's no reason for you to become paranoid. I've never seen you like this."

Tiana came out of her trance, her eyes meeting his. "I'm sorry, baby, you know I just like to be perfect with my career."

"Nobody's perfect, babe," Justin said.

"How's Taylor?" she asked. Not forgetting to act the part of a concerned parent.

"She's taking things pretty hard. I don't know what's gotten into her, but she's convinced that you hate her. Maybe you should try and talk to her again."

Tiana shook her head no. "I'm not sure if that's such a bright idea."

"You're her mother, what would be better than that?" Justin questioned.

"She tried to fight me last time. I don't know the little girl she's become."

"That's just the thing, baby. She's not a little girl anymore. Taylor's a teenager. Children change when they go from babies, to toddlers, to teenagers, to adult children. You know that. All things have a season."

Tiana went back into her trance and started back biting down on her thumb nail. "Do you think we are only for a season?" she said with a distant look in her eyes.

"Baby, you are my wife. We are together as long as we both shall live. Now I want you to stop worrying about that deadline. Call the company back and tell them you can't do it this time." Justin was firm and serious.

"Okay, you got it," Tiana said.

The doorbell rang. Justin left the room and descended the stairs. A few moments later, he called for Tiana. She snapped out of her trance long enough to walk to the door. Angela was standing in the foyer.

Tiana sighed. "This girl just won't give up," she mumbled.

"Can I talk to you for a minute?" Angela asked.

"It's late and I'm tired. Can this wait?" Tiana asked.

"It will be really quick, I promise. I won't keep you longer than five minutes."

Reluctantly, Tiana made her way downstairs.

"It's been a long time since we ran, let's do it in the morning," Angela said.

"Girl, the last thing I feel like doing is running," Tiana said.

"Oh, come on, you could use the exercise."

Tiana turned her nose down at Angela. "What you trying to say?"

"Hey, I'm just calling a spade a spade." Angela chuckled. "Come on now, it used to be your favorite thing to do before starting your day."

"Maybe another time."

"Seriously, you're going to leave me hanging on the run? I would ask what's gotten into you, but I'm afraid of the answer."

"Good, you should be."

Angela frowned. That response was not what she expected. "Well, if you decide to change your mind, I'll be on the same trail we run all the time."

"Yeah, okay, you have a good run for me."

Angela turned toward the door and left. Tiana stood in the foyer and watched her walk to the car. Angela reached her car and turned around. They both stood still for a moment in a stare down. Angela knew something was up, and Tiana pondered getting rid of Angela. Finally, Angela threw up her hand and waved goodbye.

Tiana nodded and watched her back out of the driveway.

Warm arms enveloped her and Justin's voice tickled her ear. "What was that about? You love to run."

"Are you snooping in on our conversations?"

"I always snoop." He chuckled.

"Maybe I should go running. Who knows? Maybe it will release some of this tension."

"I know what will," Justin said.

A grin crossed her face. She turned to him and they kissed. He lifted her and took her upstairs. Justin was gentle with her like he always was with his wife. He pulled off her shirt and tossed it to the floor along with her jeans, panties, and bra. They made passionate love for hours on end, Tiana basking in the glow of their wicked exchange. It empowered her to be in Justin's arms. It gave her energy to have him weak for her sex. He gave her all of him, not holding anything back, and she'd made it up in her mind that it was rightfully hers.

By the time they finished, they were both exhausted and promptly fell into a slumber. Tiana with an evil, conniving smile on her face.

# Chapter Nine

The world flew past Angela in a blur as she ran with every ounce of strength in her. Things in her love life wasn't so great and she had no one to talk to about it. Her relationship with her best friend was fading, and she had to get down to the bottom of her change. Angela knew people went through midlife crises, but this change was so drastic Angela couldn't stand it. She wanted her friend back and she would do what she needed to in order for that to happen.

Her ponytail swayed back and forth with every step she took. She had gotten halfway down the six-mile trail before she decided to stop. Sweat slid down her face and her chest as she heaved in and out. She knew why this run felt particularly hard for her today. It had been weeks since she last ran. It wasn't the same without Briana. Angela sat down on a park bench and thought about how she should begin to find out what was up with her friend. Whenever she flat out asked Briana, she would snap at Angela as if she couldn't ask her anything.

At the same time, Briana and Tiana bent the corner from opposite directions. Briana parked on the left hand side of the street, while Tiana parked on the right. Being identical wasn't the only thing the twins had in common. They could feel each other's emotions and sometimes had the same thoughts.

With the new memory Briana had received, she was ready to get out and run. She remembered loving it and needing it in her regular routine. Tiana, on the other hand, rarely ran, but when she did, she always felt refreshed. Tiana got out of her truck and bent over to tie up her shoe laces. She stood up to stretch and saw Angela staring across the street in the opposite direction.

Tiana followed her line of sight and froze when she saw Briana. Thoughts of killing them both right then and there danced around in her head, but she couldn't do that now in broad day light. Angela's look was curious she couldn't tell if she was seeing Tiana or if Briana had changed her mind and decided to come run with her. Thinking quickly, Tiana took off running toward Angela and grabbed her arm, bringing her focus toward her.

Angela snapped around when she felt the hard tug.

"Come on, girl, you dragging. I know it hasn't been that long since I ran with you," Tiana said and took off running.

Angela ran after her. "Hey, I didn't see you pull up. I thought I saw someone across the street that looked just like you. I'm seeing double!" Angela laughed.

Tiana stopped running. "Where?" she asked.

Angela turned back around but saw no sign of Briana. "That's funny," she said. "She was right there a minute ago. Looked just like you, too. Are you sure your sister is not in town?"

"If she was, what would she be doing here?" Tiana asked. "Girl, you trippin'. Come on, let's finish this run." Tiana turned back around and ran.

Angela took off behind her. This trail was one Angela had run many times, but Tiana had not. Tiana slowed her pace and let Angela take over so she could run behind her. The trail took a left and the women jogged. The wind was still cool from the morning air as the trail went up a steep hill and then down. They crossed a small stream that flowed into a steady river. The birds chirped and nature surrounded them. Tiana had never felt better. The trail went through a grove. Gray squirrels, cottontail rabbits, and raccoons scurried about. A pond sat in the grove and there were bullfrogs, box turtles, and small beetles around the ruins.

"Oh my God!" Tiana yelled, making Angela stop abruptly.

Their breathing was haggard, and Tiana rested for a second, bent slightly with her hands on her knees.

"What's wrong?" Angela said, briefly resting with her hands on her hips.

Tiana pointed. "What is that?"

"It's a red fox, he's harmless. You know that. This isn't the first time you've seen him. Now you're going to tell me you're scared of him?" Angela said, finally catching her breath.

Tiana felt like the wind had been knocked out of her. She was grateful for the break. "This place is beautiful, I appreciate it every time I come," Tiana said, even though this was actually her first time seeing the grove. "I should've brought my camera. This would've been perfect for a few shots."

"I agree," Angela said. "How's the photography thing going anyway?"

Tiana huffed, uninterested in answering Angela. She looked up, admiring how the small forest shaped the area and left an open blue sky.

"Do you want to finish this run?" Angela asked.

"Yes, let's go."

They took off again, running past rose bushes and different assorted flower arrangements. The trail made a right and went around a slope. Tiana felt like this run would be the best part of her day.

"Be careful, don't forget about the drop," Angela said.

"What drop?"

As they rounded the corner, Angela turned and grabbed Tiana just in time. Tiana slid and fell to the ground, landing on her butt. Before her was what looked to be a ten foot drop down to a lake.

"Jesus!" Tiana yelled.

"Are you okay?" Angela asked with concern.

Tiana didn't respond. Instead, she perched up on her knees and looked over the cliff. If she would've fallen off, there would've been no coming back. This would be the perfect accident for Angela, she thought. It would be too easy. Tiana formulated a plan.

"Briana, are you okay?" Angela repeated.

"Yes," Tiana said and smiled. "Very much so, thanks for saving me. I almost met my maker."

"Well, we don't want that, now do we?" Angela said. "You're going to have to get it together, sister, I can't have you falling off cliffs. The police will swear I tried to kill you."

"Why would they think that?" Tiana asked.

"Because we run this trail all the time. We know about this cliff. They would make me their number one suspect."

"How would they know we ran this trail all the time?"

Angela thought for a minute. "They're the police. I'm sure they'd figure it out."

Tiana stood up and the girls jogged off. Back at Tiana's car, Angela asked if she wanted to grab breakfast.

"Sure, I don't mind," Tiana responded.

"Can you drive me to my car?"

"Maybe you should walk, it would do you good to lose some weight," Tiana responded.

Shocked, Angela's face turned upside down into a frown.

"I'm just playing," Tiana said.

"Oh, so you got jokes?"

Tiana's phone rang. She took it out of the glove compartment and saw that it was Justin. "Hey baby."

"How's the love of my life?" he responded.

"Just finished my run with Angela, and now we are about to pick up something to eat."

"Oh, so you did decide to go run with her?"

"Yes, it was refreshing."

"You guys should do that more often," he said.

If it was one thing Tiana couldn't stand, it was Justin trying to push her off on Angela. Didn't he realize by now she just didn't want to be around her like that. That's okay because when she got rid of Angela then she wouldn't have to fake being her friend any longer, and that would be one less headache she had to worry about. Besides, she had more important things to do. Like get rid of her sister.

If she waited too long, Briana might get her memory back, and then all hell would break loose. "You're right, baby," Tiana said. "What are you up to?"

"On my way to a business meeting with an associate at J & R Firm. Our clients are going before the same judge on the same day, so we need to get ready and be on the same page. I didn't call to keep you. Have a good time with Angela, I was just wanting to hear your voice for a minute," he said.

"Thank you for calling, baby. Will you be late tonight?"

"Nah, I'll be there for dinner."

"Okay, talk to you later."

They hung up as Tiana pulled in front of Angela's car. "Where are we going to eat?"

"IHOP?"

"I'll follow you," Tiana said.

"I don't want to go home, take me with you," Taylor said to her boyfriend, Sean. "My mom is evil. She hates me."

"I've never known your mom to be the way you're saying she is. So what's changed?"

"I have no idea. She used to be so caring and attentive. She doesn't even ask about you anymore. We don't have girl's night. We don't do anything but argue."

"Maybe it's something she's going through. You should ask her about it."

"I don't want to ask her anything. She'd probably cut my head off."

Sean chuckled. "It couldn't be that bad."

"Says you," Taylor responded. "You don't have to live with her."

"I think you should talk to her again."

Sean turned the corner and pulled up in front of Taylor's home.

"Are you going to prom with me?"

"Who else would I go with? I thought you'd never ask."

Taylor leaned over for a kiss as Tiana pulled up in the driveway.

"What is your mom doing here? I thought she's at work around this time."

Taylor froze. "She usually is. Great, I wonder what she will say now."

Tiana walked up to the car and snatched the door open. "What do you think you're doing, young lady?"

Taylor groaned. The last thing she wanted was to get into another fight with her mother. "I was just getting out of the car."

Tiana reached in and snatched her out.

"Ow, Mom, you're hurting my arm!"

"That's not all I'm going to hurt when I'm through with you!"

"Mrs. Gable, I was just leaving and wanted to make sure Taylor got in okay."

"I'm sure you were. That's why you were kissing my daughter?"

"It was an innocent kiss."

"And how old are you again?"

He hesitated. "Eighteen."

"Hmmm, that would make you an adult and her a minor. Is that right?"

"Technically, but I just turned eighteen this month."

"And that changes something?" Tiana said, her face showing her displeasure.

"Mom!" Taylor yelled.

"I should call the police and tell them that you're a sex offender trying to lure my child!"

"Mom!" Taylor yelled again.

"There's no need for that, I'm leaving."

"Yeah, you better leave if you know what's good for you!" Tiana turned to Taylor as Sean pulled off.

"I can't believe you just did that!" Taylor yelled.

"Get in the house before I whoop the black off of you, girl!"

Taylor ran into the house, up the stairs and into her room. She slammed the door.

Tiana pulled out her cell phone and called Justin. When he answered the phone, she told him what she had just witnessed and added in a little extra.

"I think we need to send her to boarding school. I know you didn't want to go this route, but she's getting out of hand. What's going to happen when she turns up pregnant?"

"We'll talk about it when I get home, sweetheart. I've gotta go." Justin disconnected the call.

Why his wife kept pushing the boarding school issue was beyond him. Usually she would say maybe she should sit down with a counselor at the church, but sending Taylor away all together was not an option. He wouldn't have it. No boarding school could teach his child what she really needed, which was the ways of Jesus, and give her the love she needed that could only come from her parents. Besides, all teenagers went through phases in their lives. Even Justin did. Lord knows he gave his parents a run for their money, and they never gave up on him. How could he give up on Taylor? He dismissed the thought.

His wife may be mad about this one, but he would have to disagree with her. If she didn't like it, that was an issue they could address. Hopefully, his household could get back to being a nice loving quiet place. Lately everyone had been going in different directions. Things were starting to break down in their home. On top of that, Briana was avoiding her mom like the plague and missing church on a regular.

Tonight, he would sit her down to talk. It was time he got some things off his chest that he'd been holding back. He had to make sure he spoke in a way that wouldn't make Briana think he didn't support her, and hopefully she would understand.

# Chapter Ten

The Cadillac Escalade pulled into the driveway and came to a stop. Justin put the truck in park and rubbed the back of his neck. When he had meetings they could last all day if he allowed it. Most times, that wouldn't be a problem since his clients paid him top dollar, but today he'd had to cut some meetings short. While he stayed busy at work, the strong foundation that used to be his home was starting to shift. If he was honest with himself, it happened when his wife made the first drastic change. None of them saw it coming, but it didn't stop it from happening nonetheless. Many times, Justin wanted to ask Briana to slow down, if only long enough to give the family time to process one change from the next, but he didn't want her to think he didn't support her.

Justin understood that being supportive was imperative in a marriage. Wasn't Briana supportive of him when he went to law school and she stayed home to watch the kids? Yes, he was equally supportive when it was her turn, but if it had not been for Terri, Briana would've come home many nights with the house in disarray.

At one point, they talked about hiring a nanny but decided against it for the sole purpose of raising their children together. That was another reason Justin didn't understand why Briana was pushing the boarding school issue. If he didn't know any better he'd think she wanted Taylor to go away. He pondered on that thought for a moment. Could it be possible? He shook his head. Briana would never feel that way, would she?

Justin got out the truck and went into the house. Music blared through Taylor's closed bedroom door. At the top of the stairs, he checked his bedroom and found it empty. Where could Briana be now? He went to Taylor's room and knocked on the door, but there was no answer. He knocked harder, and after a second the music lowered. Heavy feet stomped across the floor then the door flew open.

The scowl on Taylor's face quickly turned gentle at the sight of her father. Tears sprang to her eyes and she hugged him tight. Justin held her just as tight and let her cry into his chest. He rubbed her back to soothe her and let her get all the anguish out. He felt horrible for not being around. Whatever had gotten into his wife lately was tearing their daughter apart. He didn't even know what to say.

"Please take me with you, Daddy."

Justin kissed her on her cheek and pulled back from her slightly. "I have meetings all week that will probably last until it's late. Would you like to stay over your grandma's house for a while?"

"Yes," she said.

"Grab some clothes, enough for a week's stay. Everything will be fine."

"What about Denise? She said her and mom have a secret, but she won't tell me what it is."

Justin frowned. "I don't know about a secret, but I'm sure it's harmless. I'll ask Denise if she wants to stay over too when she gets out of school. Hopefully, your mom is picking her up now."

Taylor guffawed. "If she is, then at least she remembers one of us!"

"What is that supposed to mean?"

"She hasn't picked me up from school all week. She keeps forgetting, so Sean has been bringing me home. Today, when she saw us outside the house she went nuts, saying she would call the police on him and everything!"

Taylor's eyes watered up again. She was huffing and puffing, practically out of breath, telling her dad about the altercation. This took Justin by complete surprise, and now he was upset.

"Get your things, I'll talk to her about it."

He never wanted his children to think he was picking sides so he tried not to show any anger or hostility when he and wife had disagreements. After Taylor got her things, they left and went to Terri's.

The click clack of Briana's heels could be heard before she was seen. The interview was a success, and she couldn't wait to share the good news with Charles.

"Let me help you with that." The dark skinned brother reached out to open the double doors for her.

"Thank you," she said. A small smile lit up her face.

"It's no problem at all, Mrs.?"

"Um, Ms. Finnegan," she responded.

He reached out to her for a handshake. "It's nice to meet you, Ms. Finnegan. "What is a beautiful woman like you doing in a place like this?"

"What's wrong with this place?" Briana said playfully.

"Only crazy people work here."

"Oh, I don't think so. I'd like to think good Samaritans work here."

"Whatever makes you sleep better at night," the handsome guy said. "I'm Michael, it's nice to meet you. I'm an attorney, have been for the past eight years."

"It's nice to meet you, Michael. I'm Gabrielle, this city's newest 9-1-1 dispatcher." She laughed.

Michael shook his head in disbelief. "I have to ask, why a 9-1-1 dispatcher?"

"It's something about helping people in need that got me."

"Ah ha, okay. Well here's my card, Ms. Finnegan, if you ever need a lawyer give me a call."

Briana took the card. "Will do, thanks."

She turned and walked to her car. After getting inside, she retrieved her phone and dialed Charles. It went to voicemail. She hung up and tried calling him again, hoping she could share the good news immediately, but no luck. His voicemail answered.

"Hey you, when you get the chance, call me back."

She disconnected the call and tossed her cell phone in the middle console. She set her purse down in the passenger seat and fastened her seat belt, then headed across town for a much needed manicure and pedicure. She figured that she might as well kill some time until she heard back from Charles. Once again, her thoughts drifted to her vacant memory. She sighed. The only person in her life was Charles. She had no one else to share her good news with. It was disheartening. She turned on the radio in an attempt to shift her thoughts in another direction.

As she pulled up to the nail salon, her thoughts returned. "Please don't drive me crazy," she spoke to herself. "Not today, not now."

She stepped into the salon and a woman greeted her.

"Hello, what wou you lie?" she asked. Clearly, English was not the woman's first language.

Briana could barely understand what she said. "Excuse me?" Briana said.

The woman pointed to Briana's nails and spoke again. "What would you like?"

"A mani pedi, please."

"You pick a color." The woman pointed to the different colored nail polishes on a stand next to the door. Briana browsed the colors. Currently, her nails were a nude color, but she was thinking of a dark Burberry color. After picking, she was escorted to a seat. The man working had a Mohawk and a nose piercing that made Briana wonder if he should've been in a tattoo parlor instead.

"Hi, I'm Simon. How are you today?"

"Doing great, actually. I just landed a new job." She beamed, grateful to be able to get the news out to someone.

"That's always good news, right?"

"Right!"

Simon reached for her hands and placed them on the table. He began removing the nail polish, working on her hands as if they were a work of art. Briana watched him, intrigued that this man worked so well and so determined. He obviously took pride in his job. Briana regretted the earlier thought she had. He didn't belong in a tattoo parlor, he belonged right where he was.

After he finished, he escorted her to a chair so he could complete her pedicure. Briana wanted to check her phone, but she hadn't heard it ring. Charles must have been busy because he had not called her back. He was at work, after all. Briana sighed.

## Across Town

"Okay, men," Chief Richardson said, "we have two people still in the house. A woman and her eight-year-old child, they are both in the right side bedroom at the top. The structure is on fire on the same side, but in the back. Black, get the hose going so we can try to maintain this furnace. Alonso, get the ladder up on the building. I'll need Finnegan and Keith to go in and get them. Get your gear, men, you'll have to force your way inside. The woman is still on the phone with emergency services, but she's too scared to unlock the window. Her and the child are in the room under the bed."

The men started to move quickly, grabbing supplies and getting to their assigned location.

"What do you mean now she wants to move!" the chief screamed to emergency services.

Before they could get things in order, the chief called Charles and Keith back over. "Change of plans, emergency services are saying the woman is in motion now, trying to make it down the hallway before the fire gets to them. She's not taking advice, so you guys are going to have go in and find them. Hopefully, you'll run right into them. Check it first, make sure it's not unlocked, if it isn't, knock the door down. Turn your talkies on and go!"

The men sprinted to the house. Keith got to the door first. Charles took out the Halligan bar, knowing the front door wouldn't be unlocked and they would have to force their way in.

Keith turned the door knob. "It's locked," he said.

"Stand back," Charles said.

He turned the Halligan around and propped it in the nudge of the door, making sure it was tightly in between before bending the tool. The door popped open.

The men took their talkies out. "We're in," they spoke into the speaker.

"Up the stairs, right side, gentlemen," the chief said. "Hurry up and get out of there."

Charles took three stairs at a time, getting to the top first. The second floor was full of black smoke, causing the men to drop down to get the best view.

"Ma'am!" he called to the woman, "we're here to get you out. I need you to yell so we'll know where you are."

There was no response. The men continued down the hall. Once at the end, Charles looked left and Keith looked right.

"Okay, man, I'm going this way. You check out the other side."

"Gotcha," Charles said.

The men split up, having no choice but to go in different directions.

"Ma'am!" Charles called out.

Still no response. The smoke was thicker on the side Charles was on, mainly because the fire was on that side. Chief said the woman was on the other side, but it was unknown now because of her movement. Charles' talkie came on.

"Finnegan!" Keith said.

"Yeah," Charles responded.

"I've got the woman, there's no sign of the kid."

Charles feet moved quicker. "What's the kids name?"

The chief came on the talkie. "Jeffery," he said.

Charles got down on all fours and crawled through smoke so thick he wasn't certain he'd be able to pursue that side of the house much longer. "Jeffery!" Charles yelled.

There was a loud crackle, and the roof buckled slightly. Sparks flew around the black smoke. Charles assessed the situation then took another look around. He spotted a set of legs laid out in the corner of the room.

"Jeffery!" Charles yelled.

No response.

His walkie came on. "Finnegan, what's the situation?" Chief yelled.

"I've spotted the boy! He's in the worst part of the house. The roof is coming down. I'm in here with him. I'm going to grab him."

"I told you not to go to that side of the structure, Finnegan!"

Charles ignored his boss. He was all for following instructions, but not when a child's life was in danger.

"Get out of there! The roof is going to collapse!" the chief yelled again.

Another loud crackle, and one side of the roof fell in. Charles moved fast, reaching for Jeffery. The boy was unconscious. He dragged him toward the bedroom door, when there was another loud crackle. Charles tossed the kid into the hallway as the roof fell, pinning him down. The smoke and debris flew in circles around his mask, and Charles had a moment of pause. With no body movement for longer than thirty seconds, his PASS device alerted that he was in danger.

The chief started barking out orders, trying to get his men assembled to go in after their fallen man.

Back inside, Charles lifted his head, took a breath and put his strength into working the broken piece of the roof off of him.

"Aaaaaa!" he yelled, lifting far enough for him to sit.

As quick as he possibly could, he leapt out of harm's way as the roof piece slammed into the floor. The house groaned and the bedroom sank, falling to the first floor. Charles covered Jeffery as the smoke and debris swallowed them in thick clouds. He took his personal breathing apparatus and held it to the boy's face. There was no way to tell if the young man would even be able to receive the clean oxygen since there was no way to tell how long he'd been unconscious. As Charles attempted to lift him, a set of hands reached down and pulled him along, giving him extra strength that was greatly needed.

"The boy," Charles said.

"The boy is fine," Blake said, covering Charles face with an additional oxygen mask.

They made it downstairs and out the door where EMS awaited them.

"What were you thinking!" Chief bore down on Charles. "You must have a death wish!" he said. "Get him over to the EMS."

"I'm alright," Charles said.

"Finnegan GET OVER TO THE EMS NOW!"

Charles gave Chief a glare, but didn't challenge him. He removed his helmet and work gloves. In the back of the EMS, he thought about Briana, and knew she would want to make sure he was okay.

"Blake, call Gabrielle for me, man, and let her know what happened and that I'm okay."

"Maybe you shouldn't tell her," Blake suggested.

"Why is that?"

"What's the point? It's going to only worry her."

"She's going to find out anyway." He pointed to news reporters that were filming in front of the house. "At least this way she won't panic, and she'll know I'm okay."

"Okay, I'll get her," Blake said.

Twenty minutes later, Briana came flying on the scene. She crossed the yellow tape, frantically looking for Charles. When her eyes settled on him, fresh tears stained her face. If she lost him, she would literally have no one. The thought made her heart swell. They were still getting to know each other, but she felt like she'd known him for a lifetime.

A police officer caught up with her. "Ma'am, you can't be here!"

"She's with me," a voice from behind her said.

That deep, masculine, hypnotic voice that drove her crazy when she lay asleep at night in her bedroom, staring at the wall, wishing he would come in and lay with her. She turned, and there he was standing over her, honey brown eyes and chocolate brown skin. Thick dark eye lashes and eyebrows. He wore his bunker gear, and the dirt and rubble stained all over it showed the evidence of his struggle. He gave her a crooked smile and winked.

"I'm okay," was all he said, seeing the worry and torment in her face.

At that moment, she knew she'd fallen for him. Something that was as fragile as love should've taken years to acquire, but no, not for her. Within the small time they'd known each other, she fallen for him, and she didn't know how to handle it. She felt herself getting ready to lash out.

She shook slightly. "You can't do this to me," Briana said.

"Do what?" he asked with concern.

"Die on me."

They stood in silence, recognizing the importance of their presence in each other's life. Briana wondered if Charles felt the same way about her.

"I never meant to die on you," he said, "so if that ever happens…" he trailed off.

"It can't happen, ever!"

Charles' face changed, and Briana couldn't quite read it. She wondered if she had gone too far. She couldn't help it. She loved him, and there was no apology to be made for it.

"If what I've said is too much for you, just let me know," she said.

He bent slightly, cupping her chin, and kissed her soft

pouty lips. Her breath caught in his mouth and her tense shoulders relaxed. Slowly, she fell into his chest as their kiss deepened. Around them, the scene had grown. People stood behind the yellow tape, watching as the remaining part of the burned house collapsed. It could not be saved.

Fire crews continued to work, and police patrolled the area asking questions. The woman had been taken off to the hospital and her son, Jeffery, had been taken shortly behind her. Their conditions were unknown. There were now three news stations all recording and telling their own accounts of what had happened, and in the midst of it all, the only thing Charles and Briana could be concerned about was themselves.

After his wife's tragic death, Charles never thought he would find a woman as kind hearted and with such a good spirit as Briana. He had already accepted the fact that he may never love again. How could he? His heart had been ripped out of his chest that night. Shredded to pieces. Yet, here he was, looking into the sultry black eyes of this beautiful woman with such a sincere soul. He wanted to be a part of her life. It was not a coincidence that they'd found each other. It was fate. God had allowed him to love again by sending such a beautiful person into his life.

Her concern for him was more than a friendly 'I wanted to make sure you were okay' and that was more than enough to let him know how she felt about him. Even so, he wouldn't guess around about it. He was going to ask her straight out, but not now.

The chief walked over. "Okay you two love birds, cut it out." He looked at Charles. "I thought I told you to go to the hospital."

Charles cut his brow at him. "I don't think so. You told me to let EMS check me out."

"Well, what was the verdict?"

"They told me to take some Tylenol and call my doctor in the morning," Charles joked.

"Very funny, Finnegan. Next time I tell you not to go in somewhere, listen to me! I'm not telling you this for my health, but for yours."

"What did you want me to do? Leave the little boy in the house?"

"It wasn't your call to make, it was mine," the chief said.

"That's where you're wrong, Chief. If I see a child lying unconscious in front of me, I'm going for them every time. There is no way I could turn my back on them to save my own butt, and if you have a problem with it, you should let me go right now."

Briana knew he was bold, but she had never been able to experience his boldness, at least not while she was conscious. It turned her on big time, and she had to calm her racing heart down.

Chief waved him off. "Don't get your panties in a bunch," he said. "None of that will be necessary. Nobody's telling you to leave a child behind, but you should still listen to me. What if the roof had collapsed before you got out of the room?"

"It did, but I'm still good."

"What do you mean it did?" he asked, arms raised.

This had caught Briana's attention also, and Charles realized he'd let that one slip.

"Don't worry about it, I'm good. EMS checked me out."

Chief Richardson gave him a stern look. "Take the rest of the day off, Finnegan."

"Fine," he said. "I can think of a better way to spend my time."

He grabbed Briana's hand and led her back to her car. "Can you meet me back at the station?"

"I can drive you, get in."

"I don't want to get in your car with this on. I need to get to the firehouse and change it out. I'll get Blake to drive me back."

"Okay, I'll be there when you get there."

He kissed her lips soft and slowly, looking her in her eyes. "I'll see you soon."

"Yeah," was all she could say.

## *Three Months Later*

Briana walked into the house and gasped. A strong fragrance lingered in the air. The room was covered with red long stemmed roses as far as she could see. The keys in her hand and her handbag hit the floor. She walked through the garden of roses, careful not to crush any. They occupied space in every room.

In the kitchen, roses on the table, countertops and floor, all neatly tied together in an assortment of bouquets. Briana let out a breath she'd been holding since she walked in the front door. Slowly, she walked through the house. She'd never seen such a beautiful arrangement of roses. Could they all be for her? Of course, who else would they be for? She wondered what she'd done to receive such a beautiful gift.

Although she didn't have any girlfriends except for Stacy, a new found friend she'd met at work, she could imagine the jealousy they would feel if she could call up her best friend and squeal into the phone about these roses. She turned the door knob to her room, and there it was. More roses, on her floor, dresser, around the base of her bed. In the middle of the bed was an arrangement of pink and red roses with a card standing between them.

Slowly, she walked to the card and retrieved it. It read,

*Go to the garage.*

Briana felt chills. What was this man up to? Along with the chills came excitement and wonder. On unsteady legs, she went through the kitchen to the inside garage door. She opened it and walked out, rose petals on the steps led up to a huge item in the middle of the garage, covered with a tarp and a huge red and pink bow. Another card sat on top of it. It read,

*Remove the tarp*

Briana untied the bow and put two hands on top of the tarp. With all her strength, in one quick motion, she yanked the tarp from the gift. Rose petals flew from up under the tarp, surrounding her like a tornado of love. Her face lit up with pleasure she couldn't contain. Her hand immediately went to her chest to cover her heart. She was speechless, but what was even more incredible was what lay beneath the storm of rose petals. There in front of her sat two Kawasaki Ninja sports bikes. One blue and one pink, and they were beautiful. Briana's mouth dropped open.

"I hope you love it," Charles said from behind her. As quick as a whip, Briana turned around, mouth still agape. He was standing there holding another bouquet of red and pink roses. He chuckled. "By that look on your face, I'm guessing you do?"

Briana blinked. "Are you kidding me? I love!"

Charles strode to her and stopped right before her. "And I love you," he said, his voice deep and dreamy. "And I don't want to live another day with you being my wife."

Briana's eyes grew. "What are you saying?" she asked.

"Will you make me the happiest man alive and be my

wife?" He pulled a crystal clear box from the center of the bouquet and opened it.

Another gasp escaped Briana's mouth. It was a fourteen karat strawberry gold diamond engagement ring. Tears clouded Briana's eyes, assaulting her vision.

"Oh my God!" she cried. "I love you, I love you so much!" she said. "Yes! Yes! Yes! Of course I will marry you!"

He kneeled down. After placing the bouquet on the floor, he slid the ring on her finger then lifted Briana and twirled her around. He pressed his forehead against hers and kissed her deeply, dancing with her tongue, her tears becoming one with his face. She put her arms around his neck and jumped his bones, wrapping her legs around his waist. He walked toward the house, carrying her inside and shutting the door with his shoe. They kissed and moaned in each other's mouths, enjoying the taste of lips, tongue, chins, face, and necks.

Charles kissed her on her eyelids, nose and cheek bones; they caressed each other's back, arms, and chest. Charles continued to the bedroom. Once in the hallway, he stopped in front of his door and pulled back, giving her the chance to give him her acceptance.

"Go ahead," she said.

He went into his room and laid her on the king size bed. Shoes, jeans, shirts, blouses and socks went flying across the room. Once Briana was down to her pink Victoria Secret panties and bra set, she stopped. He took in the sight of her beauty and couldn't look away.

"I want you to do the rest," she said.

Charles bore into her with his handsome light brown eyes. He couldn't believe she'd been hiding all this beauty behind those clothes. He stood back and outlined every intricate detail of her body.

After another long second, Briana started to feel a bit embarrassed. "Is there something wrong?" she asked.

"Of course not."

"Okay?"

He got down on his knees before her. "As much as I want to make every nerve ending in your body tremble, I want us to wait until we get married. I want our first time to be as sacred as our vows."

Briana didn't know what to say. This was the last thing she thought Charles was thinking. After all, it had been her who'd stopped him every other time they seemed to be taking things too far.

She smiled. "Why am I so blessed to have you in my life?"

"Why ask why?" he said with a grin.

"You're right." Charles gave her body another slow assessment. He was trying not to renege on what he'd just said, but he wouldn't. He knew she would be worth the wait.

"I love you," he said.

Briana gave a dreamy sigh. "I love you too."

He stood and pulled her into his arms. They hugged and kissed softly. "Let's go shopping," he said.

Briana's eyes sparkled. "Yes, let's!"

# Chapter Eleven

*The Next Day...*

"Girl, that rock is so big! That man really loves you," Stacy said.

Briana beamed. They were getting married in two months. Over the last couple months, Charles and Briana had grown closer than ever. Briana found things she loved like new favorite movies, favorite cities to visit, favorite songs, and favorite dishes, and Briana had even adopted some of Charles favorite foods. Many nights they'd lain awake on opposite sides of the bedroom walls, willing the other to come in and take advantage. Neither of them wanted to cross that line. Even though their chemistry was obvious, every time the opportunity for them to be intimate with each other arose, they managed to get a hold of themselves and calm down.

As much as Charles wanted to claim her, he wouldn't ever push himself on her, and he wanted their wedding night to be special. He knew that waiting until that night would mean more to her than anything, so that was his plan.

"You have a real life Cinderella story, girl," Stacy said.

"Don't I know it? I kind of feel bad, though, because I haven't introduced him to my family."

"But you don't know who your family is. That's not your fault."

"I know, but still it feels crazy."

"Well, you better get over it. There are many women who would like to fall in love like you did. He's a true knight in shining armor."

The ladies giggled. Briana was happier than anything. The relationship with Charles had blossomed over the few months they'd known each other, and their feelings had no doubt grown into love.

Stacy had been a 9-1-1 dispatcher for eight years. She'd grown into a close friend and had taken Briana under her wing and showed her the ropes. For that, Briana was thankful. Having a good friend, any friend for that matter, was good.

"I feel like I've known you all my life," Briana said.

"You know when you meet someone who is right for you, it always feels that way," Stacy said.

"You sure said that," Briana said, thinking about Charles.

Stacy continued to analyze the ring. "Girl, did he go to Jared?"

They burst into laughter. "Actually, the box said Kay Jewelers."

"Kay, Jared, they're all the same, right?"

"Not really, but I see what you're getting at."

"We should celebrate! Tonight, I'm taking you out, girl, so tell that fiancé of yours not to make plans because you're on my time."

"I don't know about that. He might have plans of his own for us?" Briana said.

"You might be right, but just in case, tell him anyway and see what he says."

"Where to?"

"I don't know yet, but I have a few places in mind. And I get to plan your bachelorette party."

"Oh no, I won't be doing that. There is no need. I don't want to see any man naked other than Charles."

"Oh honey, please. I still cannot believe you guys haven't been intimate, but it's cute though."

"Cute? Girl, I've had to have some serious strength trying to keep my hands off that man. But I want it to be right."

"Seriously, though, it will make your relationship that much stronger. You guys will be in love when you first make love, and that's always a good thing."

"What time is it?"

"One o'clock."

"I've got to call Charles. He's taking me to lunch."

"Remember to tell him we're having ladies' night, and I'll make sure to get you back in one piece."

They laughed.

"Will do."

The next two months went by in a blissful haze as Briana enjoyed and thanked God every day for bringing such a wonderful man like Charles Finnegan into her life. Today, she was feeling extra thankful, and what she had in mind as a wedding gift would be perfect. Walking into the strip club, Briana felt as if she floated on air. A Caucasian woman looking like she was about 25 came from the back wearing a two-piece bikini set. Her jet black hair flowed straight down her back and she was wearing purple fingernail polish. A tattoo of a stripper pole ran down her right arm with a woman spread eagle in red, striking a pose.

"Are you here to audition?" the woman asked.

Clearing her throat, Briana responded, "Um, no. Is the owner of the place here?" she asked.

The woman turned her head to the back. "Steve!" she yelled.

A heavyset white man walked from the back. He was bald on the top with hair running along the sides of his head. Briana wondered for a moment why the man didn't just go ahead and cut it all off. To her, the half bald look was absurd.

"Can I help you?" Steve asked.

"I hope you can," Briana said. "I'm newly engaged, and I want to do something special for my fiancé on our wedding night."

Before Briana could finish, the man started barking out prices for private shows per head of each dancer he had available. "I got some girls that might make your man not come home," he said jokingly, trying to sell her on the dancers.

"I'm sorry. I think we have a misunderstanding, I'm wanting to rent your building out for a few hours so I," Briana pointed to herself, "can dance for him. I don't want any dancers, I will be his dancer and he will be my audience."

A smile crossed the man's face as he gave Briana an appreciative once over, looking at her from head to toe. Satisfied that she was in great shape, even better than some of the girls he'd just bragged about moments earlier, he nodded and said, "How many hours will you need it and between what times?"

"Between eight pm and ten Saturday night."

"That is my busiest night, and some of my best hours." The man rubbed his jaw. "How about this? I have a private VIP room in the back. It has its own entrance and stage. You can rent out the room between those hours if you'd like. Follow me, I'll show you the space."

Briana followed the man to the back, upon entrance she

glanced around. The room was big enough for a small party. The stage was the perfect size and the seating lined the wall and circled around the room. There was also a small bar in the corner.

"It has its own sound system so the music up front wont interrupt the music in here."

"How much?"

"Seven hundred dollars."

"Great!" Briana said, elated. "Do you mind if I stop by throughout this week to brush up on my routine?"

"Not at all," Steve said.

"How much extra?" Briana waited.

"That's on the house, but I'll need the money no later than Wednesday so I can make the arrangements."

Briana took out her wallet and wrote the man a check. "It'll clear before Wednesday," she said.

The days leading up to the dance were exciting for Briana. She was looking forward to surprising Charles, and often she thought about how shocked he might be. Briana recruited Stacy, telling her she needed her to escort Charles to the club blindfolded. She didn't want him to know what she was up to until the music queued.

It was a week before her wedding and Briana was feeling jittery. Thinking about her debut on stage, she drove herself crazy, hoping Charles would like it. As if conjuring him up, her phone rang with Charles number displaying on the screen.

"Hey sweetie," Briana said.

"Hey, love of my life. Can you meet at One in Midtown? I'm running late, but I'll be there when you get there," Charles said.

"The restaurant?" Briana asked.

"Yeah," he responded.

"I'm on my way."

She got in her brand new Mini Coop that Charles had gotten her as a gift. At first she wouldn't take it, but when Charles explained to her that was the car he met her in and the significance it had to their relationship, she had no choice but to accept it. According to him, it was the same color, make, and model. Traffic was heavy around this time. It was the lunch crowd, Briana was sure of it. She found a parking spot in the back next to a company vehicle.

As she walked toward the restaurant, she hit the alarm and it chirped twice. At the front of the building, there was a line waiting to get in. Briana hoped Charles had made reservations because she definitely wouldn't be able to wait for a seat and get back to work in an hour.

As Angela drove down the street, she passed the popular restaurant, One, which was crowded as usual. She spotted a familiar face standing in line and did a U-turn. If she'd been caught, she more than likely would've gone to jail. Midtown was too crowded for U-turns, but Angela had gotten used to it. When she made it back around, the line had moved and the woman she thought she saw was no longer standing there. The same thing happened to her the day when she ran with Briana. She decided this time she had to know if she was going crazy, or if she was really seeing Briana's twin, Tiana.

She doubled parked in the back and said a prayer that her car wouldn't get towed. She moved past guests standing in line and was stopped at the entrance.

"Ma'am, the line is back there."

"I know. I called in an order, I'm not looking to sit."

The man let her through, but the restaurant was so crowded, where would she start? Angela decided to go where they would wait for the takeout orders. While standing there she scanned the restaurant. Could she be losing it?

"Ma'am?" a lady behind the bar said.

"Yeah," Angela responded.

"What's the name on the order?"

"Ummm," Angela hesitated then she spotted her.

"You know what, I'll be right back. I just saw someone I know."

Angela walked toward Briana. The closer she got to her the slower her steps became. Angela looked her over. She seemed genuinely happy. The guy she was sitting with was hot. Angela wondered whose man he was because Tiana never got her own man. Briana's hair was pulled up into a curly bun. Her curls bounced around as she laughed and enjoyed her conversation. Angela noticed there wasn't a tattoo on the back of her neck. She frowned, this was more than strange to her. She didn't like the unsettled feeling that coursed through her body. Finally, she was close enough to speak out.

"T-Tiana?" she stuttered.

Briana and Charles looked up at the same time. "I'm sorry, who are you looking for?" Charles asked.

"Tiana," she said, pointing to Briana.

Recognition hit Briana's face. She remembered Angela from the small piece of memory that was recovered the night of the crash.

"Angela?" Briana said. "How do I know you?"

Angela was taken aback. Was this girl seriously going to act like she didn't know her? Sure, they'd never gotten along before, but this was foolery.

"So you don't know me now?"

"Where do you know me from?" Briana asked, seriously inquisitive.

Angela laughed and shook her head. "You know what, forget it. I thought I saw you the other day at the trail where me and your sister always run, but then you disappeared. Now I see you here and you act like you don't know me. Why would I expect anything different from you? Goodbye."

Angela turned to walk away.

"Wait!" Briana said, rising from the booth. She took tentative steps toward Angela.

Angela turned back to her.

"I'm sorry, I don't really know who I am, so I can't tell you if I know you or not. But if you wait for a moment, maybe I can explain because I've been looking ..."

Charles placed his hand on Briana's back to calm her down. "What she's trying to say is she was in a car crash that was so severe she lost her memory. She doesn't know who she is, her family, or anybody else from her past. So she's not trying to be rude, she just doesn't know who you are, but we've been hopeful that one day she would find out."

Angela was shocked. "Oh my God." Immediately, she took out her cell phone and dialed Tiana.

"Hello," Tiana answered.

"I'm standing in front of your sister. She doesn't remember who she is. She's been in a bad accident. I need you down here asap."

A shockwave ran through Tiana. "Where are you?" her voice now sounded alarmed and dark.

"I'm at One in Midtown."

"Ask her is her number the same, if not, get it from her and send it to me in a text. I'll call her in ten minutes. I need you to meet me at my job so you can take me over there because my car is in the shop."

"Or they could just follow me over there," Angela suggested.

"No!" Tiana yelled in a panic. "The office is busy today with some top clients roaming throughout. We'll just meet them back at the restaurant."

Angela wavered. "Okay, I'm on my way," she said and snapped her phone shut.

"Her car's in the shop, so I'm going to pick her up. Everything's going to be okay. Your family thought you moved out of town, so no one's been looking for you."

Briana covered her chest. "But why wouldn't I call them? Why wouldn't they check on me? Why would I move away?" Briana had so many questions.

"You do things like that all the time, so no one was alarmed when you disappeared." Angela paused. "I talked to your sister and she said you'd moved to Cali. She can answer more questions than I can."

"I don't know if I was going to or not, but I never made it," Briana said.

"She has your number, or do you have a new one?"

"I have a new one." Briana rattled off the number.

"Okay, I've got it."

"Thank you so much," Briana said.

"No problem."

Angela left the restaurant and ran to her car. Luckily it had not been towed.

When Tiana's phoned beeped, she stored the number in her phone. Pacing back and forth, for a moment she'd freaked. Now she had no choice but to get rid of Angela.

Tiana's cell phone rang. "I'm on the fifth floor, take the elevator up."

"Okay," Angela said. "Did you talk to her?"

"Yes, and she's hysterical. At first I thought she was lying when you called me because Tiana likes to have attention."

"Tell me about it, if I hadn't been in front of her, you wouldn't have been able to convince me otherwise either," Angela said. "The elevator isn't going up to the fifth floor."

"Get off on the fourth and take the stairs."

Angela moved from the elevator and went to the stairwell, "I'm going up now." Angela entered the fifth floor and took in her surroundings. "Weird," she said.

"What's weird?" Tiana asked.

Angela walked toward the elevator. Its doors were open and all she could see were the cords that held the elevator. She looked to her left and right. There were plastic sheets hanging in various places.

"The fifth floor is under construction. Where are you?" Angela said.

"Turn around."

Angela closed her phone and turned around. "What's going on? Why are we up here?"

"Because you couldn't mind your own business, this has to happen."

"What are you talking about?"

"Let me ask you a question, Angela. Have you accepted Jesus Christ as your Lord and Savior?"

"Is that a joke?"

"Do I looked amused?"

"You already know the answer to that. What is going on, Briana?"

"I am NOT Briana. I'm Tiana, you dumbass!"

Angela's eyes were so wide they almost popped out of her sockets. Her mouth fell open.

"Woo, it's so good to say that!" Tiana said. "I've been

pretending to be Briana for so long I forgot how it felt to say my name!" She laughed eerily.

It all started to make sense to Angela, her sudden changes, the tattoo, the cold shoulder she received.

"That's right, put it together," Tiana said.

The elevator started to descend.

"You are sick!" Angela said.

"Yeah, and you're dead."

Tiana snatched the cell phone out of Angela's hand and pushed her so hard, Angela lost her balance and fell back into the elevator shaft. Angela reached out faster than the speed of lighting and managed to grab Tiana by her wrists, pulling her forward. Tiana hit the floor, hanging halfway with Angela in the elevator shaft. Tiana cursed.

"Don't do this, Tiana!" Angela screamed.

Her life was literally hanging in the balance. Fear ripped through her at the realization that Tiana was going to let her die. Tiana's lip curved up into a smile that could only be interpreted as evil.

"Please…" Angela said, just above a whisper, trying to reach a place within Tiana that had to have some compassion.

To answer her question, Tiana shook her wrist, making Angela slip even further. Her face twisted into a black mask of hatred.

"I never liked you, Angela. I never wanted to kill you, but you were too nosey for your own good, so look at it this way. I didn't kill you," Tiana growled, "you killed yourself!"

With that, she wiggled her wrist violently, and Angela's grip loosened.

"No please!" she begged, scratching the flesh off Tiana's wrist, hands and fingers, trying with all her might to hang on. "No, no, nooooooo!" Angela screamed as she fell to her death.

When she landed on top of the elevator, both of her legs broke and her neck snapped.

Tiana stood up, dusted herself off, straightened her clothes, and smoothed down her hair. Then she turned around and went back to her office.

# Chapter Twelve

Charles pulled two wine glasses from the cabinet and set them on the island in the center of their kitchen. They'd waited until the restaurant closed for Angela and Tiana to make their appearance, but no one ever showed up. Briana was in the worst of moods, and for the first time, she'd had to call her job and tell them she would be out for the remainder of the day.

Charles wanted to take her mind off of things. After popping the cork on a bottle of Frascati Italian white wine, he filled both glasses halfway, put the rest on ice, and casually walked back into the living room. With her shoes off, Briana drew her knees to her chest, wrapping her arms around them. To Charles, she looked so innocent, his heart soared for her. He wished he could save her from anything that would hurt her, but unfortunately, life was not that way. Her hair was no longer in a bun. She'd removed the clamp that held the strands together and let her dark brown curls fall to her shoulders. Briana reminded Charles of a chocolate angel. He loved her sexy slanted eyes and plump lips, the same way he loved her petite feet and curvaceous hips. To Charles, Briana could do no wrong.

He handed her a glass and she gladly accepted it, needing to drown the doubt, worry and strain that weighed on her.

Charles sat next to her and lifted her feet, placing them over his lap. "I'm sure something came up, baby. I don't think they would leave us at the restaurant for no reason after they said they would return. I wouldn't worry so much about it. I'm sure your sister will give you a call."

His voice was gentle, but deep and reassuring. Briana let out a sigh and took another sip of her wine. Charles had been trying to get her out of this funk since they'd left the restaurant, but Briana couldn't help but wonder what she could've done differently. Angela seemed genuinely concerned for her, so maybe Charles was right. Briana shook her head in an attempt to shake off the frustration that sat on her shoulders.

"You're right. She'll call." But as soon as the words left her mouth, she didn't believe them.

"I'm sorry for ruining the rest of our dinner. This is a time of celebration, and we should celebrate every moment we have with each other." Briana smiled.

Charles returned her gesture, his sexy lips curving into a lazy smile. "That's my girl," he said. "Would you like for me to warm up your food?"

"No." Briana took the last gulp of her wine. "You can pour me more of this, though."

Later that night, Briana found herself unable to sleep. This time it wasn't because she wanted to be in the bed with Charles, but because she couldn't fathom a reason for her family to stand her up at the restaurant. After four am, she finally drifted off, but at seven am sharp, the shrill of her alarm clock woke her up. Briana rolled over and tapped the snooze button. Ten minutes later, the alarm went off, and again, Briana rolled over and tapped the snooze button. When it went off the third time, she finally turned it off, but instead of getting out of the bed, she fell back to sleep.

Fifteen minutes into her slumber, a sharp tap came to her door.

Briana lifted her head. "Yes."

"Good morning, princess, can I come in?"

"Be my guest."

Charles entered the room carrying two coffee mugs. Steam ascended from the sweet aroma of decaf coffee. Briana stretched and sat up. Dressed in insulated Velcro pants, spring hooks and a cotton t-shirt with suspenders hanging from them, that did nothing to hide the muscular physique of his chest. Charles sauntered over to Briana, kissed her on her forehead, and handed her a mug.

"I thought you could use this," he said.

"You are right," Briana agreed, unable to take her eyes off of him.

She'd tried to keep her hands off this man, but he was so deliciously created that if for any reason she couldn't, she wouldn't hold herself responsible for her actions. The fact that he was sexy as all get out in his fireman uniform let Briana know she was in for a real treat when she finally let him have his way with her.

"Are you going to work today?"

"Yes, of course. I know it doesn't look like it right now, but I had a hard time getting to sleep last night." She gave him a soft smile.

Charles took a sip of his coffee and set his mug down on her nightstand. He sat down on the bed and gently pulled her into his arms. He stroked the side of her face for a second before placing his lips on hers and kissing her like she didn't have morning breath.

As their lips parted, he said, "I love you."

Her heart jumped, forming knots in her stomach. "I love you too, baby."

She lay her head on his shoulder and rested it for a moment. Charles rubbed his hand up and down her back, caressing her. Briana shivered under his touch. It was still electrifying and soothing at the same time.

"Where have you been all my life?" he asked.

Briana lifted her head and looked into his piercing gaze. Butterflies fluttered in her stomach. "I could ask you the same thing."

They kissed again, and this time, neither of them came up for air. Briana set her mug down as they continued to kiss. Her arms went around Charles' neck. His hands roamed up under her small knee length nightgown, stopping at her breasts. When his bare hands caressed them, Briana opened her mouth in shocked lust. He slid off the bed to his knees and laid her back. His long body covered her midsection and his mouth found her areola. A gasp left her lips. *Make him stop*, a voice in her head said, but she couldn't.

Briana reached down and caressed the side of his face, letting him lick and suck on her rosebuds until she felt like she was about to burst. *Make him stop.* Charles lifted the nightgown and tossed it. Briana lay before him in only her panties. Her beautiful body a sight to behold. He rubbed her and put his mouth on her sex. Her panties were thin, and she could feel the heat from his mouth. Briana wanted to wiggle out of her panties and let him have his way with her, so what was she waiting for? They were getting married, right, so why not?

As much as he loved her and as long as he'd gone without

any sex, it was obvious he would take their lovemaking to new heights.

His phone rang, but he ignored it. Once it silenced, it started up again.

Briana sat up on her elbows. "Maybe you should get that."

Charles didn't take his eyes off of her. "Maybe," he said, resting his chin on her sheer panties.

Briana arched an eyebrow and watched as he took his cell phone out.

"I'm on my way," he said, knowing it was his supervisor at the firehouse.

"I need you now, Finnegan, we're moving to Jasper road. It's an eight story building and I need all the manpower I can get."

"I'm on my way," Charles repeated and disconnected the call.

"Emergency?" Briana inquired.

"Unfortunately," he said, rising to his feet and pulling her up with him.

They embraced and kissed. "Have a good day at work, okay, and try not to think about your sister. When you least expect it, she'll call."

He kissed her forehead, then her lips, then the back of her hands one at a time.

"Don't forget, I have something planned for us—for you actually, tomorrow night," Briana said.

Charles lit up with a charming smile. "I wouldn't dare." He winked and left the room.

"I wouldn't worry about it if I were you. If it's meant, she'll call you," Stacy said.

For the better part of an hour, Stacy had tried to convince Briana that Tiana would call, but as the time went by, each minute felt like forever.

"If I were you," Stacy said, "I would focus on that fine specimen of a man you've got at home. I mean, I could never understand how you feel waking up from a coma and not knowing who your family is, but I've got to tell you, the man upstairs is watching over you because you couldn't have come out in a better situation."

She was right, this much Briana knew.

"Now, you've got a ceremony to get ready for and a show to put on afterward, so you need to put yourself in check asap. Stop thinking about who is not there for you and start appreciating who is. I know you lost your family, but you've got a new one, girl. Including me."

Briana let Stacy's words sink in. Stacy sat across from her at Starbucks, her short bob complementing her oval face, deep set eyes and long eye lashes.

The dimples in her cheeks appeared at the amused look on Briana's face. "I assume from that look you feel better?"

Briana let out a small giggle. "Yeah, you're so right, and now that you mention it, I'm nervous.

"About what?

"About everything, the wedding, the dance. Being someone's wife, I mean what do I know about being a wife?"

"Girl, I am excited!" Stacy said. "That man is going to go nuts! If he doesn't, I would be totally surprised. It sounds like you've got pre-wedding jitters. It's normal and happens to everyone. Listen, you're going to make a wonderful wife, and your dance is going to be the icing on the cake." Stacy licked her fingers as if she was licking on icing.

"I was having some issues with this dance when I first practiced." Briana shook her head. "Girl, let me tell you.

Wednesday, I went in and he had some Lil Wayne playing on the speakers. I asked him if he could turn it off because I had my own music in mind. So, I go and get changed, and next thing I know he's peeping around the corner saying he's going down the street and he's going to lock me in. Really, I'm cool with that because I didn't want him there anyway watching me practice."

"Was he watching you?" Stacy asked.

"Not exactly. I mean, whenever I looked up he was doing something, walking to the back, at one time it looked like he was trying to fix the air conditioning unit, but he could've just as easily watched when I was focused on the routine."

"This is true," Stacy said.

"So, when he left, girl, I turned up as they say." She laughed again. "You should've seen me trying to swing around that pole!"

They laughed together. "Oh my God, tell me you didn't fall," Stacy said.

"I didn't, but my swing wasn't right either, so I kind of got stuck in midair."

They laughed harder. Stacy had to scoot her chair back to bend over and laugh. Briana shook her head, tears coming to her eyes.

After a minute, Stacy was able to compose herself. "I hope you got it right now, girl, because it just won't be right if that happens after the ceremony tomorrow night."

Briana still had a smile plastered across her face that reached her ears. It was the day before her wedding and the last week had been fun and torture at the same time, trying to get the dance routine down.

"I'm good now, at least I think so. You'd be surprised how much YouTube tutorials work."

Stacy shook her head and laughed. "Well there's no time like the present to find out."

"I need you to help me get ready, then go to the house and pick him up. Let him get in the car then blindfold him. You're going to have to walk him in with the blindfold on and sit him right in front of the stage. We have our own room and it will be set up for him."

"Mmm hmm," Stacy said agreeing with Briana, "it sounds like you've got everything figured out."

"I hope so. Cross your fingers, girl, here goes nothing!"

Vecoma at The Yellow River

Stacy stepped into the room and closed the door quickly behind her. "How do you feel, girl?"

"I'm nervous again," Briana said.

"I thought you might say that, so I brought you a little something." Stacy handed her a glass of rose wine. Briana took a huge swig. "Gentle, girl, you know if you drink wine too fast it'll give you a buzz."

"That's what I need, a buzz."

"No you don't. You need to be clear headed. The last thing you want is to go stand in front of your groom drunk. He will notice, as he notices everything with you, and then you will not be able to execute your dance tonight!"

"You're right," Briana said.

"Of course I'm right. Now give me that glass back. You're supposed to sip, young lady. You look beautiful, and everything is ready. I'm glad you guys chose to get married at Vecoma, it's gorgeous outside."

"Really? That's a relief, especially since I had to put it in the hands of a wedding planner."

"What's wrong with that? People use wedding planners all the time."

"Oh, it's fine if you don't have a family to put it together for you."

"Oh, stop that! You're not about to do that today. So you don't have family that you can remember, all of your friends are downstairs and I'm here."

"You mean all of my co-workers I had to invite in order to have any guests at all."

"Are you going to mess up your day by throwing this pity party, or are you going to straighten up and go marry that handsome man downstairs? You know the one who rode in on his white horse and saved your life." Stacy let that sink in before saying, "I envy you, you know."

Briana arched an eyebrow. "And why is that?"

"Girl, if I could forget my mess of a family and marry my prince charming I would be delighted!" They burst into laughter. "You're sitting up here whining about not knowing who your family is, but what if you got the worst of families? Did you ever think about that?"

"Not really."

"Well, maybe you should. All things work out for the good of those that love the Lord, and God works in mysterious ways. He could be saving you. You better be grateful, now perk up!"

Briana gave her a sheepish grin. "Thanks."

Stacy smiled. "You're welcome. I meant to ask you, are you going by Tiana or still Gabrielle? I know you said Angela called you Tiana the day she saw you in the restaurant, so I wasn't sure."

"Gabrielle," Briana said. "I don't even know who Tiana is, and in the memory I had, she called me Briana." She tossed her hands in the air. "All I know is Gabrielle, so that's what it will be."

"Good." Stacy looked at her watch. "Okay, girl, it's about

that time. Now I'm going to get in my position. I need you at the door in ten minutes. Will I have to come back up here and get you?"

"No, I'll be ready," Briana said.

"Please don't make me come back and get you. If you break this man's heart, I'm going to kill you myself!" Stacy left the room mumbling, "All the women in the world who're looking for a good man and you're sulking."

Briana giggled. She took in a deep breath and stared at herself in the mirror. She was about to be Mrs. Finnegan, for real. She smiled and felt giddy on the inside. Stacy was right. She was one of the lucky ones. She took another deep breath and turned to the door, then opened it and stepped out.

"Okay, Gabrielle, all you need to do is make it outside," she told herself, but her feet wouldn't move. Most people had someone to help them through this process. Even someone to walk them down the aisle. "Come on, you can do this," she said.

Outside under the gazebo, Charles stood next to Blake and Chief Richardson. He'd decided that since Gabrielle didn't have blood relatives to attend the ceremony, then he wouldn't put any of his family next to him. Of course they were in attendance, his mom, dad, two brothers, his sister, two cousins, and an uncle. Blake's wife was unable to attend due to their daughter being sick, but he'd gladly stood next to his good friend on his wedding day.

They'd decided to keep the wedding small. Since it was about him and Gabrielle, his family had understood his choice to make her feel more comfortable by not having them in the wedding. Even though Gabrielle had argued and told him he was being silly, Charles didn't even think twice about it. Standing opposite of him waiting for the bride to take her place were her new friend, Stacy, and her boss. They both were dressed in yellow and white and held yellow and white carnations in their hands. The ceremony had been designed with bright yellow and white flower arrangements all around.

Stacy's eight-year-old daughter came down the aisle tossing yellow and white rose petals. Stacy beamed. When the young girl made it to her mother, she hugged her and took a seat. Next, came Blake's six-year-old son with the rings on a yellow and white pillow. He smiled ear to ear, happy to be the center of attention, and walked down the aisle faster than he should've. The guests in attendance laughed.

The wedding march cued and everyone rose to their feet. Charles took in a big breath and smiled, waiting anxiously for his bride to appear. After a few seconds with no sign of her, his smile began to falter. He looked over at Stacy and she gave him a reassuring nod. After a few more seconds, there was still no sign of Gabrielle. Everyone waited patiently. Charles could see Stacy getting skittish. He looked back at her, and Stacy lifted the bottom of her dress and proceeded to go after her. She didn't get one foot off the gazebo before Gabrielle appeared.

Charles breathed a sigh of relief. He had never laid eyes on anyone so beautiful in his life. The fact that her beauty matched inside and out was a win, win; that almost never happened. He was blessed indeed. Briana walked toward him. A white veil covered her face, hanging down to her bare shoulders. She was dressed in an white haltered Vera Wang wedding dress that hugged her body down to her knees then sprouted into a sheer layer of lace fabric.

From her end, all she saw was Charles standing in his Armani double breasted suit that fit his muscular profile so well; it was as if it was custom made for him. Briana didn't know what had taken her so long to make it outside. Looking at him now, she knew for a fact she was blessed beyond measure. They would build a lovely family together and he would get a second chance at happiness.

Briana smiled brightly and stepped to the altar. She glanced at Stacy and winked. Charles reached out and helped her onto the gazebo. Fresh tears gathered in his honey brown eyes. Briana wanted to kiss his moist lips, his skin so perfect, clean shaven and clear of all blemishes.

"You are so beautiful," he said.

"And you are so handsome," Briana replied.

She let out a breath. Everything was perfect. The sun was setting; a beautiful orange glazed the sky. The lights strategically placed around the ceremony slowly lit, casting the wedding party in a soft glow. Everyone took in the beauty of it all. There were collective gasps throughout.

Charles held on to Briana's hand and watched her as she watched everything around her come to life. His heart beat at a methodical pace. This was the day he never saw coming. Like a beacon of hope, she'd landed right into his life. He traced the details of her face like he always did.

He couldn't believe there was someone in the world who looked identical to her. Her family still had not reached out to her. As much as he tried to keep her mind off of it, his mind stayed there. He'd made a promise to himself to get to the bottom of it. If everything turned out right, he would reveal his findings. If not, he would never mention it, as if he'd never gone looking. What would be the point of breaking her heart if her family was not good for her? No, he wouldn't because he loved her more than he loved himself. He would go to extraordinary lengths to make sure she wasn't hurt.

He pulled her close and her eyes landed back on him. She smiled and touched the sides of his face. This moment was enchanting, and they were enjoying every minute and every second of it.

The pastor cleared his throat. "Are we ready?" he asked.

"Yes," they said, united.

"Dearly beloved, we are gathered here today in the sight of God and the presence of these witnesses to join these two people in Holy matrimony, which is commended to be honorable among all men; and therefore is not by any to be entered into unadvisedly or lightly—but reverently, discreetly, advisedly and solemnly.

"Into this Holy estate these two, Gabrielle and Charles, now come to be joined. If anyone believes this couple should not wed, speak now or forever hold your peace."

The silence stretched out as long as the golden sky that still glowed above them. Not even the night sounds made a peep during this sacred moment. Charles and Briana kept their eyes on each other, a smile playing around both of their mouths as they knew no one would say anything.

"Who gives this woman to be married to this man?"

"I do!" Stacy said.

The pastor turned to Charles.

"Repeat after me"

Charles spoke to Briana. "I, Charles Finnegan, take you, Gabrielle, to be my lawfully wedded wife. I vow to love you and care for you as long as we both shall live. I take you with all of your imperfections and your strengths, as I offer myself to you with my imperfections and my strengths. I will support you when you need support and turn to you when I need it. I choose you this day as the person I want to share eternity with."

A tear ran down Briana's face and Charles gently wiped it away then placed the ring on her finger. Briana took her ring and repeated her vows to Charles. She slid his ring on his finger, smiling at him as his eyes glistened with tears.

"By the power vested in me, I now pronounce you husband and wife. You may now kiss your bride!"

Charles removed Briana's veil. They leaned in and kissed, sealing an eternal bond. The wedding party cheered as the photographer took pictures.

"Ladies and gentlemen, I present to you, Mr. and Mrs. Finnegan"

Rose petals were thrown at them as they finally pulled apart to turn and smile at their friends and family.

"Congratulations!" Charles' mom, Sherri Finnegan, said. "Honey, you are the most gorgeous bride! I am happy to have you as part of our family, and I can't wait to steal you away for mother daughter shopping sprees!"

"Give me some time with her first, Ma, then I might let you borrow her."

They laughed.

Charles' father walked up. "I'm proud of you, son." Charles gave him a nod. "Here's to your new family."

Charles Finnegan Senior handed his son an envelope. Charles knew it was cash, probably more than what was necessary. He grabbed Briana by her hand and planted a kiss. "Welcome to the family, daughter, I hope you don't mind me calling you that."

Briana was in heaven. It was surreal to be in the midst of people who truly felt like family to her. "It's no problem at all," she said.

"Are we headed to the restaurant?" Charles Senior asked.

"Yes, we'll meet you there."

"Okay."

"With one last pat on the back, Charles Senior and his wife turned and walked away as Blake and Chief Richardson gave Charles their congratulations.

"I'm so happy for you!" Stacy said, squealing with delight.

She slightly pulled Briana away from the men. "I knew you could do it. I was ten seconds away from coming upstairs and dragging you down by your ankles."

They both laughed.

"I knew you were, I just had a moment."

"Girl, you had several moments! I'm glad you came through, though. Poor Charles looked like he was about to start sweating bullets." They laughed again. "Are you coming to the restaurant for the reception?" Briana asked.

"Of course, I wouldn't miss it for the world because who's going to get your groom back to the strip club if I don't?"

"Good point," Briana said.

# Chapter Thirteen

At the restaurant, Briana and Charles sat with smiling faces across from their wedding party as Blake and Stacy exchange flirtatious banter. They'd been going at it ever since they walked through the door, and Charles knew for sure that Blake was drunk. If his wife knew he was here flirting with another woman, she surely would drag him by his ears out of there. Charles shook his head.

"Alright that's enough, you two are having too much fun."

Briana shook her head up and down in agreement. "I think he's right," she said.

"Oh come on," Stacy said. "It's just a little harmless fun, nobody's hurting anybody."

"Not yet," Briana said.

They laughed.

"Somebody else has to have fun besides you guys!" Stacy said.

"Not really," Briana countered.

They laughed again.

"Wow, really, Gabrielle, and why is that?"

"It's our night, we're supposed to have all the fun."

"And what fun you will have!" Stacy said, giving Briana a knowing look.

Charles looked from Briana to Stacy. "Anything I need to know about?" he asked.

"It's a surprise," Briana said.

"Is that so?" Charles said.

"Yes, and I need this young lady to sober up!" she said, shooting daggers with her eyes at Stacy.

"Hey, chill out, honey, I got you! I haven't had that much to drink."

"The problem is you don't drink at all, so even a little to drink can have you drunk!"

Stacy looked from her wine glass to Briana and back to her wine glass again. "You're right," Stacey admitted.

"You are making me weak!" Briana said.

"Okay, I'm done. I won't be taking another sip. I need to make sure I come through for you." Stacy pierced Briana with her eyes. "I will come through for you."

Charles held his hands up and waved them around. "Hold up, what's going on?"

Briana and Stacy turned to him simultaneously. "What?" they both said innocently and burst into a fit of giggles.

Their silent secret threatened to spill out over the glasses of wine they'd both consumed.

"Listen, listen," Stacy repeated. "You shouldn't drink anymore either, because seriously, you need to be right yourself."

Charles removed his arm which lay smoothly behind Brianna. "We got secrets already?" he said.

With the sexiest look she could muster, she turned to him. "Of course not."

Charles couldn't even come back with a rebuttal; his woman had entrapped him. If being with her was like this, she would have him wrapped around her fingers all the time.

"Trust me, man, you want to wait and let this surprise happen!" Blake said.

Briana whipped her head around, her eyes popping out of their sockets. She turned to Stacy, who had a sheepish look on her face. "You told him?"

"Un huh, told me everything, too. It's okay, your secret is safe with me," Blake said with a toothpick hanging out his mouth, his eyebrows jumping at Briana.

She smacked her hand against her face. "Oh my God, I can't believe you did that, STACY!" she yelled.

Stacy shrunk in her seat. "It kind of just slipped out."

"Is it that bad?" Charles said. "You've really got my interest piqued now."

Briana huffed. "I'm going to the ladies' room, and when I get back, we're leaving!"

"Gabrielle, you're not mad are you? I'm sorry I let it slip, I didn't mean to. Hey, girl, chill out. I still need to sober up a bit."

"Well you better be good and sober by the time I get back! Shame on you, Stacy!"

"I guess this wouldn't be the best time to put my two cents in," Chief Richardson said.

Briana gasped, sharply mortified. She fixed Stacy with a look of contempt. "Oh, don't worry, she didn't tell me, Blake did."

"Oh, well, since it was Blake, that makes it so much better," she said, with sarcasm dripping from her voice.

Stacy stood. "Come on, Gabrielle, be nice!"

Briana gave her a stern look then turned to Charles. "Excuse me, sweetheart." She reached down and caressed his chin.

He smiled up at her and let her pass.

Stepping away from her wedding party, Briana made her

way to the bathroom. She passed a couple of men who smiled and winked as she strode past them. She'd changed out of her wedding dress into an all-white knee high bandage dress, which hugged her curves at every angle. When Charles first saw her in the dress he couldn't take his eyes off of her. It was when he blinked that he told her she would be by his side all night to keep the wolves away, and boy was he right. The way men were looking at her now, you'd have thought she was Little Red Riding Hood on the way to Grandma's house. She wondered if Charles was watching her. She tossed her hair and looked back, smiling bright. He was looking. Hard. She blew him a light kiss. He winked and blew a kiss back.

She turned back just in time to push the swinging door to the bathroom open. After she finished in the bathroom, she washed her hands then played with her layered hair, shuffling it around. When she got Charles to the strip club, she wanted to look her most daring. She pumped herself up as she stood there, trying different poses. Arching her back, giving herself a little preview before getting comfortable enough to realize she had the dance down.

"Okay," she told herself. "Here goes nothing, or should I say, everything."

She shook her head at the fact that she was even talking to herself. Walking back through the swinging doors, she made her way back to her wedding party. Another man sitting at a corner table whistled.

Briana looked his way slightly before doing a double take. Her steps paused, a smile spread so far across the man's face you'd have thought he'd won the lottery, but it was not the man who had grabbed Briana's attention. Instead, it was her own face that stared back at her, a smirk lining the woman's mouth. Sitting at the booth behind the man was her twin, clear as day.

Tiana held two beer bottles in her hands. She set one down and opened the other, sliding it across the table from her in a silent invitation for Briana to come sit down. She popped the top on her own beer and took a swig.

A rush of emotion ran through Briana. Her eyes stretched the length of her cheek bones. Could it be at this moment when she needed her family most, on her wedding day, she'd been given the gift she'd always hoped for? There were so many questions she wanted to ask, but her legs were officially sand, weighing so heavy she hadn't moved, her feet glued to the ground.

From across the room, Charles glanced her way. Seeing his wife's demeanor, his smile faded and he followed her line of sight. He stood abruptly when he saw Tiana sitting at the far end table. Before he could make strides to get to Briana, her hand raised, stopping him in his tracks. She needed to talk to her sister, and she needed to do it alone.

Tiana crossed her legs and relaxed in her chair. Briana found her footing and on unstable legs made her way across the room. When the man at the booth realized Briana wasn't looking at him at all, he mumbled something unintelligible and left his seat.

Standing in front of her now, Briana searched every part of Tiana's profile. Her jet black hair lay relaxed in layers very similar to Briana's. The same set of sultry eyes, full lips, sleek nose, and long neck aligned her face. Her ruffled black blouse teased men with cleavage peaking from the first two open buttons, her body curved inward giving her waistline a small shapely outline before peaking over curvy ample hips. Her jeans fit like a glove and her black four inch Manolo Blahniks finished off her sexy look. Briana also noticed the wedding ring on her left hand and black pieces of jewelry that accessorized her ears, neck, and wrists. At the same time Briana assessed Tiana, Tiana did the same, except hers was a quicker assessment.

"Sit down, I won't bite. Not this time," Tiana said.

Briana sat slowly, taking in a quick unsteady breath at the sound of her own voice. She knew twins could be identical, but what were the odds that their voices were the same?

"Weird, isn't it?" Tiana said, reading her sister's mind. "I know. I don't like it too much either."

Briana was unsure and unsettled about this visit. Something about her sister was odd, she couldn't put her finger on it. "It took you long enough to come over here," Tiana said. "I see congratulations are in order." Her manicured nails sang a tune against the cold, wet beer bottle as she lightly tapped against it. "You know, you always find the right ones, sis. You… always, have them eating out of the palm of your hands."

There was something about the way she said it. Almost as if she was bothered.

"Unfortunately, I have no idea what you're talking about," Briana said.

"Why are you playing this game? You know who I am, you know who your family is. If you want nothing to do with us that's fine, but don't play games with us," Tiana said.

Briana's eyebrows furrowed, causing wrinkles that could only be brought to life by confusion. Her arms spread, her fingers turned into fists, then relaxing, she stretched them.

It was Briana's time to sit back and cross her legs. "You can't be serious," she spat.

Tiana tickled herself. Briana was a fidgeting fool. Tiana didn't come here to play around with her, but it was fun. The fact that she'd actually gotten married was funnier. As it was, she was a bigamist and didn't even know it. "Oh, I'm actually quite serious."

"This is not a game, this is my life! Why would I do such a thing? As a matter of fact, I tried to get in touch with you through um," Briana snapped her fingers, "what's her name, Angela? We waited for you at the restaurant and you never showed up. Why would I do that if I was playing games?" Briana held out her hand to stop Tiana from responding. "Listen, I don't know who I used to be or what type of history we have, but I would love to start over. I honestly have no idea about my past, and if you don't believe me you can ask my doctor."

Tiana turned her head to the side. "You're seeing a shrink?" she asked.

"I mean, my healthcare doctor. He can confirm everything I'm saying."

"There's no need to do all that."

"Why didn't you show up to the restaurant that day?" Briana asked.

Tiana folded her hands, her fingers intertwined. Her thumbs rubbed together and her foot bounced slightly. "My best friend died."

Briana let out a sharp gasp. Both of her hands flew to her mouth. "Angela?" she said.

Tiana bobbed her head up and down, confirming the answer.

"When? How?" Briana stumbled with her words. Tears clouded her eyes and she quickly wiped them away, but not before Tiana noticed.

"Are you crying?" she asked, her voice showing no sign of remorse for her fallen best friend.

"I know it seems silly," Briana said, "but I feel like I knew her."

She looked down at her trembling hands and dropped them to her lap, giving Tiana a tiny smile before trying to shake off the traumatized feeling she had.

Tiana evaluated her. "How is it that you feel like you knew her?" she asked.

"I had a dream, or a memory. The doctor seems to think it was a memory."

Tiana's eyebrows shot up. "What was this memory about?" she asked, her voice sounding agitated.

"Um, well, I've had two memories about her, actually. One we're running through a beautiful grove. I have no idea where, but call me crazy, I actually tried to find it one day."

"Did you?" Tiana asked.

"Um, no." Briana opened her hands in her lap, and with one hand fidgeted with the palm of her other hand.

Tiana tried to keep her voice neutral, but she was beyond aggravated.

"What was the second memory about?"

"Um, well one day my husband and I, who was my fiancé at the time, were leaving the grocery store when we caught a flat tire and ran off the road into a pole. I was in and out of consciousness when Angela appeared again. We were on our way to a lawyer's luncheon or something."

"The first time you had the memory, did it come from nowhere or did something happen like the car accident?" Tiana asked.

"It happened within moments of each other."

*That's it, she has to go for sure,* Tiana thought. The fact that she was regaining her memory only meant it wouldn't be long before she remembered everything.

"Do you remember anything else?"

"Justin," Briana said.

Tiana's stomach turned into a knot. "Justin?"

"Yeah, I don't remember who he is, but I remember his name showing up on my phone as me and Angela were on our way to the luncheon. I figure we must have the same friends since she was your best friend," Briana said.

Tiana wanted to reach across the table and cut Briana's throat open. She could feel what she considered an invasion to take back what Tiana had worked so hard to attain.

"Can you tell me who Justin is?" Briana asked.

"Unfortunately, I can't," Tiana said through clenched teeth.

"Are you sure?" Briana asked, noticing the steely look she was now getting from her sister.

"Why would I lie to you if I could? Do you remember me being a liar?" Tiana said.

Taken aback, Briana shook her head. "Of course not."

Tiana turned her beer up and chugged the rest. It was not enough. She needed something stronger. "Check this out," Tiana said. "I would like for us to start from the beginning as well. We should get together sometime and go for a run. I know exactly the place where the grove is located. We should go there, since that's the spot you remember. Maybe it will help you trigger the rest of your memory," Tiana said, as if she really wanted to get to know her sister.

Instead, she remembered the drop off the edge that Angela had saved her from. She would toss Briana over that cliff kicking and screaming if she had to.

Briana, now smiling, said, "Of course! Oh my God! Thank you for the invitation!" She jumped up and slid in the booth next to Tiana, throwing her arms around her neck and squeezing her tight as small tears ran down her face. She was overjoyed that she would be able to be a part of her family and get to know her sister again.

Caught off guard by the sudden reaction, Tiana leaned away from her sister, her eyes bulging. Her hands still rested on the table, wanting to push her sister to the floor. Slowly, she placed her arms around her sister's waist, realizing she should play this out if she wanted it to go in her favor.

A fake grin spread across her face. "It's no problem at all," Tiana said, wanting to throw up in her mouth.

"When should we get together?" Briana said, finally letting Tiana go, but not moving from her side.

Tiana took a breath. The closeness of her sister made her light headed. "How about tomorrow?" she said, wanting to get rid of her sister as soon as possible.

"Unfortunately, tomorrow I'll be on my honeymoon. I just got married, remember?"

Briana's happiness was making Tiana even more aggravated. It's like the stars were aligned in her favor. "When would be the best time for you, big sis?" Tiana said.

"Big sis?" Briana inquired.

Tiana blew air to the wind. "Yeah, you are two minutes older than me."

Briana beamed. "Ah snap. Now you will have to do as I say!" she joked, but Tiana did not at all find it comical.

Briana had no idea how much Tiana loathed her, had no idea how much of her life was spent in Briana's shadow, had no idea how much Tiana just wanted a life of her own, a look of her own, a man of her own, a good one too, not just any man.

"I want you to meet my husband!" Briana said.

Tiana shook her head side to side, "I don't know if that's a good idea."

"What? Why not?"

"I don't want to intrude on your celebration."

"Intrude? I just spent half an hour over here talking to you."

"Which is all the more reason why I should just beat it, so I can let you get back to your hubby."

Briana waved her off. "Don't be silly, he's wanted to meet you ever since the day we saw Angela in the restaurant."

Tiana put her hands up in protest but Briana wasn't hearing any of it.

"Come on, let's go," she said scooting out of the booth with Tiana's hand. She practically dragged her out of her seat. "Besides, I'm the oldest. I told you, you'll have to do what I say." She snickered.

Tiana almost hit her over the head with her beer bottle, an empty bottle that she'd been holding on tightly to ever since her sister had invaded her space. As they made their way across the restaurant, Charles having watched their full exchange, stood to his feet like the gentleman he was, prepared to greet them. Following suit, the rest of the men at the wedding party also stood.

Every man in the restaurant had turned their total focus toward the twin beauties. A double dose of every man's dream as they practically drooled, tongues hanging and tails wagging. Even the men sitting with a wife, girlfriend, or companion had their attention focused on the women. They walked in stride, their bodies screaming sex appeal, hips and curves beckoning to be treasured and highly favored. Briana in her bandage dress and white five inch stilettos, and Tiana in her black ruffled blouse, skin tight blue jeans, and four inch black Monolo Blahniks, which came from Briana's closet, made even some of the women's head turn. It wasn't a coincidence that their hair had similar styles, straight and long, in layers right past their shoulder blades. Their steps aligned as they pulled up to the table.

Tiana plastered on a fake smile as Briana slid her arm into Tiana's. "Everyone, I'd like you to meet my twin sister," she said.

"It's nice to meet you, twin sister," Charles said.

Tiana rolled her eyes in a playful banter. She held her hand out to shake Charles'. "Hi, I'm Briana."

"Briana, that's a lovely name."

"Very beautiful indeed," the other men agreed.

Tiana almost rolled her eyes in disgust.

"So your sister's name would be?" Charles asked, wanting to hear it from her twin. "Tiana," Tiana said.

"It's okay, it's aight," Blake joked.

"Oh hush," Briana said. "It's just fine if you ask me." She swatted at him.

Tiana looked from Briana to Blake in silent fury. That was another thing she'd had to deal with growing up. Her sister had the better name. She inhaled and exhaled slowly. Her eyes roamed the wedding party as everyone introduced themselves. She took in Stacy, Briana's new best friend, looking like an office secretary in her conservative dress and modern black rimmed prescription glasses. She took notice of her dimples. Cute, she thought. Her hair was in a long sleek ponytail and she wore black two inch no brand name heels. When her eyes landed back on Charles, she noticed he was watching her. Calculating, he was evaluating her, trying to figure if she was friend or foe.

Immediately, Tiana liked him, he was her cup of tea. Strong jaw line, goatee, chocolate glazed skin, a low haircut shaped to the outline of his head. Sharp and sexy, and also observant. She would watch him, but she was sure he would watch her. Who knew, maybe he wanted to see just how much like her sister she was. As they watched each other, a smile spread across her face. It wasn't just any smile and Charles knew it. It was more challenging, daring, devious, dangerous, exotically so. He could tell she was the precarious twin just by her presence.

"You guys look too much alike, it's crazy!" Stacy said. "Oh, I'm so glad you decided to show up tonight, it's the best thing you could've done for your sister. She was so worried about you not showing up at the restaurant, and I tried to tell her not to worry about it, and look, here you are. What did I tell you, huh?" She said, turning from Tiana to Briana.

"Yeah, yeah, you told me."

"Unhuh, don't yeah, yeah, me, and yes, I did. I told you alright. You should have a seat and stay for a while. I'd love to tell you about Gabrielle's… I mean Tiana's gift for her hubby," she said, batting her eyes.

Briana's eyes bucked. "Oh shut up, Stacy, haven't you told enough people already?"

"Well, I know you'd want your twin sister to know, right?" She beamed and her eyebrows danced.

"Don't do that thing with your eyebrows. You look crazy," Briana said.

"Actually," Tiana said, finally taking her eyes off Charles.

Everyone stopped chatting, interested in what Tiana had to say, and amazed at the sound of her sultry voice. "I've got to get going. I just wanted to stop by and surprise my big sister." Tiana gave Briana a playful slap on the back.

Briana's smile stretched from one ear to the other.

"How did you find out about the wedding?" Stacy asked.

This grabbed everyone's attention, as no one had thought to ask. Tiana cut her eyes at Stacy. She sure did talk too much, and if it was up to Tiana, she'd kidnap her and cut her tongue out of her mouth. "If I tell ya, I'd have to kill ya," she pretended to joke.

Everyone snickered, but the smile on Tiana's face was more than playful. It was sinister, and Charles was keenly aware of it.

### *Two Hours Later…*

Charles checked his image in the mirror. He didn't know what to expect and he didn't know what his dress code should be. All day he'd thought about Briana and her surprise. He eventually came to the conclusion that it was probably dinner and some type of romantic comedy at the movies. However, that was kind of the normal thing to do. Stacy made it sound as if it were a real treat. Whatever it was, he would just relax and enjoy it.

Tonight, he decided to dress casual. This was his third outfit change since the wedding. He wore dark blue jeans and a blue and white button up Calvin Klein elbow length short sleeve shirt. The collar was folded back and the top two buttons were left open. On his feet were his icy white air force ones and his hair cut was fresh from Lou's Barber shop. He put his hands up to his mouth and blew to make sure his breath was fresh, even though he'd brushed his teeth for the third time and sprayed a dash of peppermint oral spray for the second time. In each ear, a small round diamond earring sat.

After getting a good look at himself, he placed his hands in his pockets and smiled. Content with his appearance, he went into the living room and grabbed the bouquet of red roses and a thin rectangular box. Even though Briana thought she was surprising him, which she was, he also had a surprise for her.

A horn blared outside his door. He took one last look around and went out, locking the door behind him. He opened the door to Stacy's white 2014 Ford Explorer and got in.

"Good evening, Mr. Finnegan," Stacy said.

"Good evening yourself," he responded.

"You look nice," she said, but that was an understatement. Of course, Stacy couldn't really tell him he was drop dead gorgeous, but she was sure he already knew.

"You think so?" he said, looking back into a mirror. "I hope Gabrielle feels the same way."

"I'm sure she will. If you don't mind, my instructions were to blindfold you until we got there."

Charles guffawed. "You're playing right?"

"No, I'm not." And to prove her point, she held up a satin black blindfold.

Charles' eyes bucked, entertained by the secrecy of it all.

"If she wants to play this game, I guess I'm up for it."

"Trust me, you'll be glad you did," Stacy said and reached over to put the blindfold on Charles.

He grinned, his white teeth turning his already sexy face into a mysterious racy expression. Stacy had to remind herself this was her friend's man.

Twenty minutes later, they pulled up in front of the strip club, Exotic Encounters. As Stacy led him in through the VIP door and to his seat, she got a look at the set up and giggled to herself.

"Hey, no laughing unless I get to see," Charles said.

That just made Stacy giggle harder.

"Okay," she said, "my work here is done. You guys have fun." And with that, she pivoted and left the building.

Seconds later, Charles heard what sounded like heels click clacking across the floor until the sound was right next to him. He could smell a thick vanilla fragrance in the air.

A hand gently touched his shoulder. "Are you comfortable?" came her sultry voice.

"I am," he responded.

"Good." Briana bent down and placed a soft sweet kiss on his lips. They tasted of chocolate cherries.

"Mmmm," Charles moaned. "Can I take this blind fold off now?"

"Not yet, count to ten then remove your blind fold."

As Briana took her place on stage, the beat dropped and Beyoncé's "Dance For You," began to play. Charles removed the blindfold and got his first look at his surroundings. In front of him was a stage with a mirrored background and two poles on opposite sides, with enough room in the middle for dancing. He sat up, taking it all in. Red and white rose petals decorated the stage floor, and sitting on a stool with her back to him, Briana moved slowly and sexually to the beat.

She turned, giving him a peek of her face. Her back arched and bucked as she slowly danced to the song. When she stood and turned toward him, his body responded to her sexiness. His mouth parted and profanity slipped off his lips.

Briana threw her leg up on the stool and gyrated her hips. She was wearing an all-white spaghetti strap baby doll lingerie set that held her breasts up and out in a tight grip and flowed halfway down her hips, stopping right at her white thong. Accenting her legs were white see through pantyhose, white straps, and a garter belt that clung to her. Her hair was long, hanging down her back in a bunch of exotic curls. She turned and sauntered to the pole, letting each step accentuate her hips as they rotated. She stretched to grab the pole as high as she could before doing a quick spin with her legs spread. She'd perfected that swing, and the sexy way she slid down the pole to a stop had Charles on his feet and at the stage. Briana danced as if the choreography was made for her and not Beyoncé.

Beyoncé sang,

*"Loving you, is really all that's on my mind and I can't help but think about it day and night I wanna make that body rock sit back and watch. Tonight I'm going to dance for you O wo oooo."*

Briana dipped her hips and rocked them side to side, swaying with the song. Her arms draped over her face as her hips did another jiggle. She bent over and swung her hair, turning to the side and easing into the sultry back dip as Charles watched her.

He wanted to grab her so bad, but at the same time, he didn't want her to stop. She had turned him on in every way imaginable. His loins were screaming for her body and he didn't want to deny himself the pleasure of her. Briana had taken a bold step with this surprise, and he knew he wouldn't be able to hold himself back much longer, come hell or high water.

Briana went back to the stool and continued the dance, swirling and twisting her hips. Swinging her hair and going to the other pole on the other side of the stage. He watched her intently, forgetting to blink, his eyes glued to her every motion. Briana had seen lust in his eyes before tonight, but the way he was looking at her now made her shudder with instant arousal. His deep gaze penetrated her flesh, sending shockwaves of erotic sensations through her.

She sauntered back in front of him for the end of the song. Her hands roamed up her thighs to her breasts, behind her neck and she bucked and swayed to the sound before going back into her back dip that had her body waving at him, beckoning him to come and get her.

Just as the song was coming to an end, Charles reached out for her and she went to him, dropping to her knees and crawling like a lioness. He grabbed her and pulled her to him, unable to wait any longer. He pressed his lips to her mouth, letting his tongue explore the inside of her tunnel.

"Mmmmmm," she moaned.

Another song rang through the speakers. "Body Party" by Ciara, and if Charles had anything to do with it, that's what would be happening next. He pulled Briana to him, her legs encircling his waist and her butt on the stage floor. He sucked her lips and nibbled on her earlobe.

"That was the sexiest thing I've ever seen," he growled.

His hands explored her baby doll attire, running his hands all over her. "I love you, girl, and I don't want to live another minute without making love to you," he said, low and guttural.

Briana moaned in pure ecstasy, her heart hammering in her chest. "I love you too, so much."

She let him assault her with a barrage of kisses. He slid her thong down and lay her back, kissing her inner thighs. Briana shivered, her hormones out of control. He put a mouthful of her sweetness in his mouth, determined to taste every inch of her valley below. Her back arched and he placed her thighs on his shoulder as he feasted on her. She was about to lose her mind.

She grabbed his head. "Charles, Charles, baby..." she moaned saying his name as if it was her midnight mantra.

He sucked, licked and fed on her until her climax had reached the point of no return. She twisted and turned, her legs and thighs trembling as her body released its ultimate orgasm, but he wasn't through with her yet. Their night had just begun.

# Chapter Fourteen

## *Two Weeks Earlier*

A flash of lightening broke through the skyline. The clouds formed dark shadows as thunder roared like an animal in the jungle. Tiana stood in front of Angela's rose red casket. Shades covered her eyes and her hair hung straight to her shoulders. She wore a black Burberry wool blend double breasted coat, her hands resting neatly inside her pockets.

Next to her, Justin pulled her hand and gave it a gentle squeeze. Tears flowed from her eyes to her chestnut brown cheeks. Friends and family of Angela stood around them, some weeping some, still in shocked silence. The reverend was saying a prayer when drops of rain fell from the sky. The sky lit up again and the wind blew in a heavy chill.

Things had happened so fast. Before Tiana knew it, she was offering to pay for Angela's funeral. She played the part of the heartbroken friend, drawing sympathy and condolences from everyone around her. Tiana thought Justin took the news harder than she pretended to, but she was ready for this whole debacle to be over with. Now that Angela was out the way, she needed to move on to more urgent issues. For one thing if Briana wasn't a pain in her side before, she definitely was now. Somehow, she'd managed to find her way closer and closer to Tiana and her family. It was time to put an end to it. There couldn't be anymore running into her by accident.

This had become her life lately. Formulating plans to make sure anyone around her didn't threaten what she'd worked so hard for. However, when Terri looked at Tiana today, she stared her down without blinking. Even though Tiana wore shades, she could feel her mother breaking through the lenses, knowing she was not Briana. She had told her to ride with her in the limo when the service was over, but Tiana wasn't crazy. If her mother had the slightest inkling of who she was, Tiana would stay far away from her. Her acting skills hadn't failed her yet.

When Tiana and Justin arrived home, Tiana went straight to their master bedroom and stripped as she ran a hot shower. A foggy layer of steam warmed up the bathroom, wrapping around Tiana. Without saying a word to Justin, she got in, leaving the bathroom door ajar. Tiana had put on her best performance when they lowered Angela into the ground. Crying out loud, even letting out some high pitched screams. Justin had asked Terri to take the kids, and now they were home alone. Sliding the door back to the shower, Justin stepped in and put his arms around Tiana. They stood for a moment, letting the water from the blissful massage head soothe them.

Tiana was tired of pretending. She was done being mournful. Things had been rough enough on her recently. Justin had taken Taylor to stay with Tiana's parents, and what was supposed to be a week had turned in to three. That same day, Justin had questioned her to no end, firing one question after another. Why wasn't she picking Taylor up from school? What had her mind so preoccupied that she couldn't remember to pick up her own child? He had even asked if she was seeing someone else.

They had gone into a full blown argument and Tiana had never seen Justin so upset. Tiana had to dig deep within and put on her best Briana performance to get him to calm down. She told him how absurd it was that he would ask if she was cheating. Denying that she would ever do anything to hurt him like that, and she had no desire to be with anyone but him. Tiana had practically begged him to forgive her for not being there for Taylor like she should, and in the end, he had. Now, she wanted what she couldn't get enough of.

She leaned into the warmth of his chest and rubbed her backside against him. She let a small moan slip her lips, and his arms caressed her. The feel of each other's body in the wet heat had them both writhing in erotic pleasure. Justin laid kisses on Tiana's neck and shoulder; he never disappointed. Whenever she needed him, he was there. What a man, what a man, what a man, what a mighty good man, and he was all hers.

Tiana bristled in elation at the feel of him. She bit her lip as he held her closer to him, feeding her what she needed. Night after night, they'd found themselves in the throes of passion, satisfying an insatiable sexual appetite, and they didn't plan on stopping anytime soon.

## *Present Day*

On the other side of town, Briana lay in Charles arms, completely spent from another round of lovemaking. After her dance on Saturday night, Charles had tried to make love to her right there on the stage. It had taken a lot of promising for him to reluctantly wait until they got back home. They couldn't get in the door quick enough before Charles was all over her. Briana hadn't stopped him. She welcomed his hungry craving and found herself giving him the same thirst he gave her. They did finally make it to the bedroom, and by the time they made it, they were both naked.

Briana had moved back on unsteady legs, trembling at the thought of his ravaging. When she bumped into the bed, she lowered herself to it and slid to the middle, spreading her legs open, giving him a full look at her beauty. When he crawled between them he kissed her lips, trailing down her neck to her luscious breasts. Her nipples were already standing at attention for him, and he took pleasure in licking and suckling on them like they would feed him the energy he needed to sex her all night long. Briana twisted and turned underneath him, she could feel the length of him rubbing against her labia.

"Charles…" she panted, parting her legs, telling him to put her out of her enchanted torture. "Charles," she begged.

"Tell me what you want?" he said.

Briana let out a whimper, her thighs shaking in anticipation.

He had all but taken her whole on the stage, and now he wanted to tease her until she begged him to put her out of her misery.

"Please…" she said.

That's all it took for him to bury himself inside her, giving her every piece of him. They cried out to each other, falling deeply in love with every kiss, suck, and breath they took.

A week had passed since then, and they were still at it. Now that they'd jumped the broom, there was nothing stopping them. Currently, Briana and Charles were in his Ford headed to Six Flags over Georgia. Charles wanted to take her out for some fun. Briana was grateful for him. Headed down I-20 west, Charles sat comfortable in the driver seat.

He glanced at Briana and caught her gazing out the window. He reached over and grabbed her hand, holding firm to her. She turned to look at him, a smile softening her already smooth features.

"We're almost there. You can see the amusement park from here, look." Charles pointed out of his left side window. The rollercoaster rides were huge, swooping up, over, and under tracing around the park.

"Do you plan to get on any of those?" she said.

"You don't?" Charles asked.

"I like the soft rides, not the ones that give you a heart attack."

Charles laughed. "How old are you again?" he joked.

She swatted at him, "Are you trying to call me old?"

"I would never do that; you're doing it all on your own."

She glared at him.

"What?"

"I'm not old," she said.

He twisted his lips, teasing her.

"I'm serious!" she shouted.

He got off the highway on exit forty-seven. "Prove it," he said.

She folded her arms. "Alright, we'll see how long you last on all those crazy roller coasters."

"Oh I think I'll do okay. Besides, I'll have you there to comfort me the whole time." He smiled and winked.

They found a parking spot and went in. The park was filled with people walking about the aisles, standing in line for food, games, and joy rides. "I remember when I was sixteen and my mom brought me and my two sisters to the park," Charles said. "Every ride I wanted to get on, my little sisters were too young or short to ride them. And, of course, if they couldn't ride, neither could I."

Briana chuckled. "I bet you were mad, huh?"

"You know it, and I took it out on them every chance I got at home, teasing and messing with them." He grinned.

"That is so wrong," she said.

They walked up to a dunking booth. The guy sitting on the seat was dark skinned and handsome. They could tell his height by his long legs. He sat smug, arms crossed, daring them to take their chances. His eyes wandered over to Briana. She waved and he blew her a kiss.

Charles leaned close to Briana. "Let me show you what I do to men that flirt with my wife."

After paying the vendor, Charles picked up a ball and stepped into his swing like a professional baseball player. The ball flew gracefully, hitting the mark with one try. The bell dinged, and the man fell into the water. Charles flexed his shoulders, his biceps dancing at his command.

Briana blushed. "Okay, I think I like that."

His smile was intoxicating. Briana was feeling an addiction to him. He pointed to the prizes. "Which one, bae?"

She pointed to sun hats and chose a brown one. As the vendor handed him the prize, Charles set the hat on Briana's head. He turned and wrapped his arms around her, pulling her in for a kiss. Briana put her arms around his neck, caressing the back of his head with her hands.

"Thank you, handsome," she said.

"Are you thanking me for a kiss, love?"

"No, I was thanking you for the hat." Briana pointed to a bunch of race cars. "Let's race," she said.

Charles arched his eyebrows. "Let's do it."

They walked to the Gold Town Racers and got in line. As they waited, they watched other couples flying around the track laughing and bumping into each other. When it was their turn to get in, Briana's face lit up. Charles loved her face, her womanly features, sexy kitten eyes, her full exotic lips and childlike laughter.

They strapped seatbelts across their waists and it was on. Every chance they got, one was bumping the other. Briana's head hung back. She laughed until tears sprang forth and a round of giggles fled her vocal cords. She'd tried to get away, but Charles made it his business to bump her. If he had his way, he'd bump her all night. After the bumper cars, they made their way over to the park grounds to cozy up under the stars and watch the park's fireworks display.

"Are you happy?" Charles asked.

"Very," Briana said, turning to him and nibbling the bottom of his earlobe.

"Good, I'm the luckiest man in the world," he said.

"And I'm the luckiest woman in the world."

"Are you happy?" Briana asked.

"Are you kidding? I just said I'm the luckiest man in the world, woman!" He rolled on top of her and she spread her legs, allowing him to rest between them. He planted a trail of kisses on her neck up to her earlobe. "I love you," he said.

"I love you too."

"How do you feel about seeing your sister after the wedding?" he asked.

Briana's face lit up. "It was good," she said.

Charles wasn't convinced. He searched her face. "Just good?" he asked.

"I don't know what I expected. She was kind of..." Briana's words trailed off. "I don't know what to call it." Charles had a word for it, but he wouldn't put any in Briana's mouth. He would let her tell him how she felt about her family. "At first she seemed kind of confrontational."

"How so?" he asked.

"She accused me of pretending to lose my memory so I wouldn't have anything to do with the family."

Charles sat up, it was almost similar to what Angela had accused her of. "Why are you just now telling me this?"

"I haven't really had a chance to talk to you about our conversation."

"Nonsense, you've had plenty of chances, baby."

"When, honey? When we were making love all day?"

He smirked. "I guess you're right."

"Of course I am."

"So what else did she say?"

"To make a long story short, she said she wanted to meet up with me at the place I had my first vision."

"The grove," they said in unison. They gave each other a lingering look. They'd only been married a short time, yet they felt like they'd been together forever.

"She says she wants to try and jog my memory since that's what I remember. I thought that was kind of her, and I want to get to know her. Really, she has no reason to lie to me. So, if we're starting over, I might as well give her the benefit of doubt."

Charles wasn't too sure about that. His gut told him her sister needed to be watched, and if it had to be by him, it would be. He didn't feel too comfortable leaving his wife with her. Sister or not, she was still a stranger to both of them.

"We haven't set a time and date yet, she wanted to do it the next day but I told her I would be on my honey moon."

Charles grinned. "Did you plan a honeymoon I knew nothing about?" he asked.

"No, but I wasn't about to go anywhere with anybody the day after we got married, so if being at this park constitutes being on our honeymoon then so be it! I only want to spend time with you for now."

"Trust me, we will have our honeymoon."

He rolled back on top of her and they kissed. Fireworks went off overhead, but all they could focus on was each other.

## *A week later...*

"9-1-1, what's your emergency?" Briana said.

"Oh, thank God someone answered the phone. I've had to hang up and call back three times!" an elderly woman said.

"I apologize, ma'am, what's your emergency?"

"My cat won't come down out of the tree because the neighbor's blasted dog got loose again, and it's time for him to eat. I don't want him to starve, and my son won't be back from Oklahoma for another week. Can you send somebody over here, please? A nice officer to help get Mr. Pickles down?"

"Ma'am, this is the emergency services. You'd have to call a place that deals with pets to help you with Mr. Pickles."

"But this is an emergency, and those places try and charge me. I'm on a fixed income, I can't afford it. Oh please, ma'am, please. It's an emergency!"

When Briana had taken the job as a 9-1-1 dispatcher, the last thing she thought she'd be doing is getting calls that weren't an emergency. As it happens, seventy-five percent of the calls weren't emergencies. She'd gotten so used to it, that when the real emergencies came through, she almost forgot how to handle them.

"Ma'am, give me your address." The woman spat off her address. "An officer will be over shortly."

"Oh, thank you, thank you so much!" she repeated and ended the call.

"Another cat in the tree?" Stacy asked, turning around from her station.

Briana shook her head up and down. "Yes, I'm going to take five. Can you watch my desk for me?"

"Of course."

Briana got up and went to the breakroom. Inside, she pulled her phone from her case and saw she had two missed calls. One from Charles, and one from an unknown number.

She called Charles back. "Hey, you," he answered.

"Hey yourself," she said.

"I wanted to see if I could fix you something for dinner tonight. Do you have any good food in mind."

"Surprise me," she said.

"Will do. How's it going at work?"

"It could be better, but mostly like always, no real emergencies."

"That makes your job easier, right?

"Makes my job boring," she said.

"We'll have some fun when you get off. I love you, get back to saving the world," he said.

"That's you! I love you too, honey." They disconnected the call.

Briana noticed the voicemail icon. She went to her dial pad and held down the number one, allowing her phone to ring her voicemail.

"You have one new message," it said.

"Hey, this is your sister. I wanted to see if we could get together sometime, say tomorrow, for that run. I'll give you call back in about two hours so be on the look out." The call ended.

Briana was elated that her sister had called, although she wondered why she didn't just leave her number. Either way, she was definitely ready to get together, so she would make sure the next time her sister called, she wouldn't miss it.

# Chapter Fifteen

Charles pulled up to the park and cut the engine.

"Babe, you really didn't have to come," Briana said.

"Yes I did."

"Honey, I'm just going to be with my sister. She's family, you would've known my whereabouts."

"That's all fine, but I'm not taking any chances with you."

Briana thought it was cute how Charles worried about her. She couldn't have asked for a better man. "Aww, baby, don't be such a worry wart," she joked.

There was a sudden tap on the driver side window. Rolling his window down, Charles looked into the eyes of Tiana. Her hair was pulled up into a clean tight bun on top of her head. She smiled, giving him a long look. "Morning, are you ready?" she asked, still looking at Charles.

He turned to Briana. She held a girlish smile on her face. It still amazed her that there was someone with her exact features.

"I can't get over how much we look alike," Briana said.

*You will,* Tiana thought. Finally bringing her focus to Briana, Tiana said, "It's something you'll get used to. Come on." She waved her over and rested her arms on the driver side windowsill. When Briana turned her back for a second to get out, Tiana reached up and caressed Charles' face then pulled her hand back and winked.

He glared at her as she stepped back off the curb to greet her sister who had just rounded the vehicle. Charles was worried about Briana. Obviously, her sister was going to be trouble, but what could he really do about it? She was family, and as it stood now, she'd done no wrong in Briana's eyes. It would take for her to notice the deception, and Charles wasn't so sure that would happen.

Briana strode up to the car and leaned in, planting her nude colored lips on to Charles' mouth. She inhaled his scent and stuck her tongue in his mouth, making his libido awaken.

"Woman," he growled, their mouths still doing a mating dance. "If you don't back up, I'll take you back home with me and have my way with you."

"Mmm," was all Briana said.

Tiana rolled her eyes. Maybe once Briana was out the way, she would try her hand with Charles. She could manage him and Justin, but poor Chris would be an afterthought.

Briana pulled back. "I love you, I'll see you a little later, okay?"

She caressed the sides of his face, her touch loving and pure, it felt nothing like her sister's.

He pulled her face in and planted a kiss on her forehead. "Keep your cell phone on you at all times."

"Baby, how am I going to run with my cell phone?"

"Find a way to do it," Charles said.

Briana sighed. "Okay, love." She smiled brightly then turned to her sister, who was waiting impatiently, tapping her toes on the curb.

"Are we ready now?" she said, exasperated.

"Sorry about that, you know how newlyweds can be." Briana still wore a bright smile.

"Of course," Tiana said, pretending to care. "Let's go. My car's over here."

"Oh, I thought we were already here?" Briana said.

"Not exactly, the grove is closer, around the corner."

"We could run there, right?"

"No, we couldn't," Tiana said matter-of-factly.

"Oh, okay. Lead the way."

They got into Tiana's Kia Soul. Briana buckled her seat belt. After all of the accidents she'd had in a car, she wasn't taking any chances. She had no way of knowing at that moment she was taking the chance of a lifetime. Tiana drove down the street for three miles and made a right turn, pulling into a parking spot at the other end of the park.

"See, that wasn't so far, now was it?" Tiana said.

"Not at all, we actually could've run here," Briana said.

Tiana rolled her eyes. "Let me let you in on a little secret. Running is your thing, not mine. Every once in a while, I will get out here and run, but not much. So for me, we could not have run here."

Briana laughed and shook her head, even though Tiana wasn't joking. Tiana checked her surroundings. As she looked into the rearview mirror, a familiar Toyota Camry pulled up two spots behind them and parked. Surprise crossed her face. "Excuse me for a minute, I've got to handle something real quick."

"Ooookay," Briana said, turning to watch her sister exit the car. Immediately, she started arguing with the woman who'd walked up. Briana cracked her window to see if she could hear what they were arguing about.

"Why are you following me?" Tiana steamed, rolling her eyes and neck at Terri Williams, the twins' mother.

"I have been trying to reach you every day for I don't know how long. I know why you're ignoring me, and I'm on to your scheme! You should be ashamed of yourself and God don't like ugly! You've got some explaining to do!"

Tiana sighed. She knew her mother knew she was not her sister. But she'd done everything she could to avoid her. This conversation was bound to happen, but it could not have come at a worse time. "I don't know what you're talking about!"

"Really, you're going to play that game with me?" Terri said. "Little girl, don't you think I would know my own children? I mean, I may be getting old, but I'm not blind dumb and senile! What are you doing in your sister's house, and where is your sister?"

"Why are you following me, and why are you sticking your nose where it shouldn't be, mother?"

"My nose is where it should be! This is the only way I could get in contact with you. Now tell me what's going on, or I'll call Justin and ask him!"

At that moment, Denise Gable, Briana's six-year-old daughter exited her grandma's car. Tiana and Terri whipped their heads toward her when they heard the car door slam.

Tiana threw her hands up. "What is she doing here!" Tiana asked.

"Don't take that tone of voice with me, young lady. I always have my grandbabies, especially since you're no kind of mother! By the way, the girls want their real mother back. They both know you're not her!"

"What are you talking about?" Tiana said through gritted teeth.

"I know you told Denise that you and her mother were playing a game, and she would have to go along with it or Daddy would be mad. She's six years old for God's sake, she tells her grandma everything. Taylor wasn't sure at first, but after hearing Denise tell me that, she threatened to run away! I had to calm her down, telling her I was sure you two girls had an explanation for this. Now what's the explanation? I'm not asking you again!"

Tiana was livid. The world as she knew it was falling apart, there was no way she could keep this charade up now. She couldn't very well get rid of her own nieces. Denise slowly and timidly made her way up.

In the car, Briana noticed her through the passenger side mirror. Struck by the little girl's resemblance, she opened the door and got out the car. When she turned to Denise, the little girl struck out running into her mother's arms. Briana dropped to the ground, allowing Denise to throw her arms around her and hug her neck. She did, as tight as her little arms could.

Briana's eyes watered. It was obvious that this little girl was a part of her family. She looked just like Briana, and she could tell she missed her by the choke hold she held around her neck.

Tiana and Terri watched the exchange. Seeing Briana, Terri pushed past Tiana, but Tiana grabbed her, stopping her in her tracks. Terri turned around, her open palm sending a smack so hard across Tiana's face that her hand itched and burned.

Tiana, unable to take the chastisement lightly, reached around and smacked her mother back with an equally stimulating hit. It caught Terri off guard, knocking her to the ground.

"I missed you so much, Mommy. When are you coming home?" Denise said.

Briana was shocked at the little girl's revelation. She pulled her back and searched her eyes, tears coming from both of them. "Sweetheart," Briana said, but before she could finish, Tiana marched over and picked Denise up.

"Denise, remember what I told you?" she said.

Denise shook her head up and down, tears falling steadily from her little face. "But I miss…" she started to say.

"Ssssshh, I know, I know," Tiana repeated with the little girl in her arms.

She turned her back to Briana and walked back to Terri's car, opened the door and put Denise in, leaving Briana squatted down in a daze. "We don't want to make daddy mad, now do we?"

"No, but I miss my mommy," she cried.

"Mommy's coming home soon, I promise, okay. In the meantime, we will make her a gift to welcome her back. I want you to think of something you want to make for her."

This seemed to lift Denise's spirits. "Okay."

Tiana kissed her cheek and strapped her back in her seat belt. She shut the door and made her way back to Terri. She glowered at her and walked back to her car.

"Let's go," she said to Briana. "We'll have to do this some other time. I'll take you back home," she said. Her plans all but ruined for the day, she had to regroup and get her thoughts together.

Like a zombie, Briana lifted from the ground and looked over at the woman who was also getting up.

"So, you're just going to let your sister do that to me and not say a thing?" Terri said.

Tiana hit the dashboard. "Let's go!" she yelled at Briana.

Briana jumped in the car and they sped off. Her head was spinning. The little girl had thrown her off earth's axis, and she felt like her world was tumbling over.

"Stop the car," she said, her voice low and controlled. When Tiana ignored her, she yelled, "STOP THE CAR!"

Tiana swerved to the side of the road and put the car in park.

"What was that?" she asked. Still dazed, her hands trembled slightly.

"It was nothing,"Tiana said.

"Nothing?" Briana said. "NOTHING? That little girl, she called me mommy." Tears filled Briana's eyes, but none fell. She turned full circle to her sister. "SHE CALLED ME MOMMY!"

"Lower your voice."Tiana glowered. "I heard you perfectly fine the first time."

"So?" Briana waited for an explanation. Now her arms were folded.

Tiana shook her head and laughed. She didn't owe Briana a thing, who did she think she was?

"She's confused, obviously. We look just alike, remember?"

Briana was shaking profusely. "I don't think she was confused. I think I may be confused."

"REALLY?"Tiana said.

"Yes, really, and who was that woman back there. She looks just like us."

"That's because she's our mother."

The tears Briana was holding at bay finally found their way down her face. "How could you treat her like that? Why wouldn't you tell me?"

"Maybe because I didn't want you to know." Tiana was shooting darts with her eyes at Briana now.

Briana was so confused.

"Did you want to meet everybody at one time? Because I thought we were trying to get to know each other first,"Tiana said.

"That was the case, but when our mom and my daughter showed up, there was a change of plans. You should've told me!"

"THAT IS MY DAUGHTER, NOT YOURS!" Tiana screamed.

She was boiling now, she would not let Briana take this family away from her, not after everything she'd done to get them and keep them. Briana opened the door and got out. She slammed it and started walking down the street. There was another door slam. Tiana was hot on her heels.

"Where do you think you're going?"

Briana took out her cell phone and dialed Charles. "I'm getting away from you. I don't know what your problem is, but ever since you accused me of playing games and wanting to be away from the family, I have been getting strange vibes from you. I'm leaving."

Tiana reached out and grabbed Briana's arm, stopping her. Briana yanked her arm free and continued to walk. Tiana's second attempt to reach out failed. At this point, she was ready to knock her over her head and drag her back to the car.

She grabbed both arms and turned Briana around. "You're acting like a complete fool right now!"

Briana slapped Tiana as hard as she'd watched her slap their mother. Blood trickled from Tiana's nose. A sharp gasp fled her mouth and her eyes bucked. There were no more words. She grabbed Briana by her throat and slung her to the ground. She got on top of her and tried to choke the life out of her.

Briana didn't really mean to slap her sister, but she was so mad at the fact that she'd hit their mother and had been keeping things from her. Briana grabbed Tiana's wrist, trying to pry her neck free of her grip. The women struggled, one losing then gaining again and vice versa.

Briana reach up and grabbed Tiana's face, clawing her nails across her cheeks.

"Aaaaaaaa!" A howl left Tiana's lips as her grip loosened and she reared back to touch her face.

With the moment of freedom, Briana rolled to her side, coughing and wheezing, trying to catch her breath. She pushed Tiana back with as much force as she could and jumped to her feet. She took quick steps away from Tiana. Her phone was on the ground. She quickly retrieved it and dialed Charles again. When he answered, she couldn't catch her breath fast enough to say anything, so he hung up. Not two seconds later, he was calling her back.

"Baby," she heaved, trying to get the words out. "Come and get me. I need you to come and get me now, please," she wheezed.

"Where are you?"

"I'm at the corner of Frazier and Columbia. Hurry." She disconnected the call.

When she turned around, Tiana was making her way back to the car. She watched her look for her keys, but she couldn't find them. Tiana searched all over and around the outside of her car before getting on her knees by the drainage and retrieving them. The car's engine revved and pushed forward. She was coming right for Briana. Briana jumped onto the sidewalk, knowing if her sister wanted to run her over, the sidewalk wouldn't protect her.

When Tiana reached Briana, she pulled the fender up to her knees and stopped. The deadly look on Tiana's face told Briana everything she needed to know. Her sister hated her.

"You know I could kill you right now, don't you?"

Briana trembled. Chills ran through her body. What had she done? She'd gotten in the car with the devil, and he was a she.

Tiana laughed, a cryptic sound leaving her lips. She

reached into her glove compartment and retrieved her three eighty handgun.

Charles bent the corner on two wheels, pulling up on Briana. She jumped in the car so fast, Tiana never had a chance to stop her. He pulled off, leaving Tiana steaming. She decided not to give chase. She didn't want to kill them both at the same time. She put the car in reverse and took out her cell phone.

"Hello."

"Hey baby, I want to come see you."

"It's about time," Chris said. "Come on over, I'm waiting for you."

# Chapter Sixteen

"Bang! Bang! Bang!" Terri knocked on the door of Justin and Briana's home, but there was no answer. She'd been calling him all day, but he was not picking up. "Where are you?" she asked aloud.

She returned to her car and sat in the driver's seat for a moment. She hadn't had a chance to clear her thoughts. Her daughter, Tiana, had been pretending to be his wife. Did he know? Why would he agree to such a thing? He was supposed to be a Christian man. Terri didn't pretend to know what went on in their sex lives, but she hoped that her daughters and Justin were not into any kind of foolishness. She pulled out her cell phone and dialed her husband.

"Hey, sweetheart, are you on your way home?"

"Gill!" Terri screamed. "You won't believe what happened to me just now!"

Terri relayed to her husband, Gill Williams, the incident between her and the twins. Even though Briana realistically had nothing to do with it, she blamed her for not helping her. "She just stood by and watched!" Terri said. "I don't know what's gotten into them. This is not like them, Gill, what's going on with our girls?"

"Calm down and take a deep breath," Gill suggested. "I'll get to the bottom of it. I want you to come home right now!"

"I can't seem to find Justin. I just don't know what to do!" Terri continued to say.

"Are you listening to me?" Gill asked. "Stop everything you're doing and come home now!"

Terri was a nervous wreck. "Okay, okay," she repeated, "I'll see you in a minute." They disconnected the call.

Gill picked up his cell phone and dialed Tiana first. The call went to voicemail. "Tiana, when you get this voicemail, you need to call your father back immediately. Don't make me come looking for you," he warned.

## *Across Town*

Briana examined the bruises on her neck in the bathroom mirror. Her neck felt tender and sore. It had been an hour since the altercation with her sister. Never in her wildest dreams had she thought their meeting would've gone down like that. It was like nothing she'd ever experienced. She thought about the fact that there was a chance finding her family would not be such a good thing, and it hurt her to think that maybe she was right. However, she couldn't shake the feeling that the little girl was her child. How could she go on with her life without ever knowing? Why would Tiana lie to her about it? It was possible the little girl was confused, wasn't it? She sighed in exasperation. She just didn't know what to think, and Charles was not making it any better.

He'd got it in his mind to file a restraining order against Tiana. He had a great point; Tiana was mental. She'd tried to choke her to death, run her over with the car, and she straight up told her she could kill her if she wanted to. What did she ever do to Tiana? She wished she could ask her straight up, but being in her presence again was out of the question. Besides the bruises on her neck, she had a bruise above her right eye. It was very light, and Briana didn't even know how she'd gotten it. She had to get out of the house. She felt suffocated in the bathroom. She needed to clear her head.

There was a light knock on the door. "It's open," she said softly.

Charles stuck his head in, opened the door and stepped in. Holding an ice pack and glass of water, he walked to her and placed the pack on her bruise right above her eye. He handed her the water and she took a big gulp.

"Thank you," she said.

He stood and watched her with glowering eyes. He was pissed. His gut had told him not to leave her, and he felt responsible for what happened to her.

"I love you," she said, watching his steely look go from menacing to warm. "I love you too," he said.

He wrapped his strong steady arms around her waist and pulled her into him. His warmth covered her back and eased around her body, putting her in a cozy blanket. "I'm sorry I wasn't there for you," he said.

"Don't be sorry, it wasn't your fault. How many times do I need to say it? There was nothing you could've done if you would've been there."

But Charles knew that was a lie. If he'd have been there he would've taken Briana home as soon as the argument between her twin and their mother began.

"I think I'm going to take a drive," Briana said.

"Where are you going?"

"I just need to clear my head," she said.

"What is it you're not telling me," he asked, turning her around to face him.

Briana hesitated. "There was a little girl," she said.

"A little girl, where?"

"She was in the car with our mother. When she saw me, she ran into my arms and called me mommy," Briana said, getting choked up.

Tears sprang from her eyes and ran slowly down her cheeks. Charles released her and took a step back. He wiped her tears with his hand.

Briana's head fell into her hands and she sobbed.

"I don't know what to do," she said, her voice broken from her distress. "My sister said it was her little girl and she was confused, but she didn't seem confused to me. She seemed very sure that I was her mom. She told me she missed me and wanted to know when I was coming home." Briana sobbed even harder.

Charles grabbed her quickly, wrapping her back in his embrace. He held her tight as she cried into his chest her tears soaking his button down Tommy Hilfiger shirt.

"What am I going to do? I have to find out, I have to know, Charles!" she was hysterical now.

"We will find out together," he said.

Briana let her emotions rain on Charles, and he took every bit of it in. He always knew finding her family would be emotional, whether good or bad. Briana collected herself and wiped her face with the back of her hands. Charles reached over and grabbed a hand towel, dabbing her face lightly with it to soak up the remaining tears.

"I need some time to think," she said. Charles understood, and wanted to give her the space she needed, but he also felt he needed to protect her; as her husband, it was his duty.

"I really don't want you driving in the state that you're in. It's dangerous," he said.

Briana knew he was right, but she had to. She gave him a

small smile. "Thank you for caring so much about me," she said. "I don't know what I would do without you in my life."

"You'll never have to find out," he said.

She wrapped her arms around his neck and they kissed softly. "Give me about thirty minutes," she said, "I won't go far, I promise."

Charles wavered, but he didn't have much of a choice. He thought about following her, then thought better of it. "Thirty minutes," he said.

Briana kissed his face and walked past him. He went behind her, walking her out the door and to the car. He opened the driver side door and handed her cell phone to her. She got in the car and pulled off.

As she drove, every thought about the day's events went through her head. The little girl's face stayed stuck at the forefront of her mind. It would haunt her in her sleep until she found out.

*I miss you, Mommy. When are you coming home?* Briana shook her head, but couldn't dismiss the little girl's voice. Her eyes began to water, making her vision impaired. She pulled to the side of the road to give herself a minute to reboot. Maybe she shouldn't have left the house. After all, Charles had been there for her through everything. There was no need to be alone now, when she needed him most. She thought about the restraining order and reached into her handbag. She retrieved the business card from the lawyer she ran into at the 9-1-1 station. Maybe she should give him a call and ask for his advice. She shrugged. What could it hurt? She put the address on the card in her GPS and followed its directions until she pulled up in front of Adler and Adams Associates.

She parked the car and got out then realized she was still dressed in her running wear. She paused and thought about changing, but she was too tired to do anything. All she wanted was to get his advice and be on her way. As she stepped into the office, the doorbell chimed.

"Good afternoon," the lady behind the desk said. "Do you have an appointment?" she asked.

"No, actually I don't. Do I need one?"

"Depends on if you're okay with seeing anyone or if you have someone in mind."

Briana handed the lady the card.

"Have a seat, Mrs.?"

"Finnegan," Briana said.

"Have a seat Mrs. Finnegan and let me see if Mr. Benton is available."

"Thanks."

She found a seat in one of the plush office chairs. The reception area was tastefully designed, with splashes of purple and gray colors in the rug, table accessories, and chairs. Even the pillows in the chairs were designed with this office in mind. The elevator doors opened and a group of lawyers sauntered out of them, having midday chatter.

"Peyton Manning will definitely be in the hall of fame. You are crazy to think otherwise," one man said.

"You can only go into the hall of fame if you're retired, and Peyton is never retiring!" The men laughed.

*Football, of course,* Briana thought. Their cheerful banter had taken her mind temporarily off of her problems.

One guy stepped around them. "Okay, fellas, I have a midday lunch with the wife."

"I thought you couldn't reach her," the other guy said.

As the two men went back and forth, Briana was having a heavy feeling of deja-vu. The guy glanced her way, then quickly turned back.

"Tiana?" he said.

Briana stiffened. There was a sudden jolt in her head,

almost like a lightning bolt. Memories poured through her head faster then she could catch them. As they ran through her mind, she tried to make sense of them all.

She stood up and gasped sharply. "Ju-Justin?" she stammered.

Justin made his way to her and frowned. Looking into her eyes confused him.

She reached up and touched his face with both hands. "My hot desire," she said lightly.

Justin's mouth fell open. His wife hadn't called him that in about two years. It was her secret term of endearment that no one else knew about. So why was Tiana saying it now? Stunned into silence, Justin thought about his wife over the past months then assessed the woman in front of him.

As a horrible revelation hit him like a ton of bricks, he took a step back. "Can't be," he said, feeling bile threatening to rush out of his mouth.

"Oh my God," Briana said.

Both of them were stuck in silence, trying to put the missing pieces together. Briana was hit with a hard bang. The memories that should have been welcomed and received with love only left her feeling despair and heartbroken. If her memory served her right, Justin was her husband. A sharp pain filled her chest. She fell to her knees, her handbag hitting the floor. Her heart broke in a thousand pieces. What had she done? She'd fallen in love with and married another man, and he was the love of her life now.

The memories that now came to her, invaded her mind like an assault rifle. Her head pounded with pain like being hit over the head with a sledgehammer.

"Briana?" Justin said.

Saying her name only proved she wasn't wrong. She looked up at him, still stuck in his own revelation. She remembered loving him and only him. She remembered their life, their love, their friendship, and their kids.

"Oh God," she said, now holding her stomach.

"What is going on?" he said. "Get up, I need to talk to you."

He looked around and all eyes were on them. Everyone in the room was obviously confused. "Mrs. Finnegan?" Michael Benton asked.

Briana looked over to him. She couldn't even gather herself, let alone her thoughts. She held her hand up and waved him off. She grabbed her handbag and cell phone as it started to ring. It was Charles. She'd been gone longer than thirty minutes, and this was his third call.

Briana pushed past Justin and ran to her car. She tossed her handbag and cell phone inside, and threw her hands on the roof of the car, leaning into the car door. With her head hung, she sobbed uncontrollably as her reality brought on more pain than she could bear.

"God, why, why, why?" she asked. "What did I do to deserve this? I thought this was a blessing, but wha-what is this?" she asked, not knowing what to do about it all. "Lord please help me!" she called out to God.

"Briana," Justin called out her name.

She whipped her head around and felt another stab of pain. She couldn't deal with seeing him right now, and didn't know when she would be able to deal with seeing him ever again. After everything that happened, she couldn't look at him in his face. She wasn't his wife anymore. She belonged to someone else, but she still loved him. Remembering their love made her heart melt and her head feel like it would explode with pain. It was sad that something so heartfelt could cause her such pain.

Justin walked to her. "I need to see something," he said.

Her body tensed as he got closer. Slowly, he turned her

head to the side and lifted her hair. There was no tattoo. He stepped back, disturbed.

"How is this possible?" he said.

She shook her head. "I don't know. I don't know anything," she said, her mind in turmoil.

"You must know something!" His confusion was turning into madness. "Tell me you got your tattoo covered up."

Briana looked confused. "What tattoo?"

Justin shook his head in denial. "No, no!" he repeated. "This cannot be happening! Why would this be happening?"

"Listen, we need to have a serious conversation," Briana said.

She gave him the short version of where she'd been for the last eleven months. The more she revealed, the more Justin turned into a madman. How on God's green earth could he have been sleeping with the wrong woman for almost a year and not know it? More alarming, why would she do it? He noticed the ring on her finger.

"That's not the wedding ring I gave you," he said, fearing what she would say next.

Tears spilled from her eyes. She was a mess. "I'm married to someone else," she said.

It crushed him with the weight of one hundred tons. She watched his heart break literally in front of her eyes. He broke down in front of her.

She went to him. "I'm sorry, I'm sorry, I'm so so sorry," she promised. "I had no idea, I haven't had any memory of my former life until I saw you just now. Seeing you jarred it for me. My full memory. I don't know what to do. I'm sorry, please forgive me," she begged.

He lifted his head, his eyes red rimmed. With a heavy heart, he said, "My love, I've been sleeping with your sister this entire time. I am the one who needs forgiveness. I thought she was you…" His words trailed off, not knowing where to take them.

Briana jumped back as if she'd been bitten by a snake. The distraught look on her face making him weaker by the second. Their lives were in utter chaos. Briana's phone continued to ring. She reached into the car and answered it.

"Baby, are you okay?" Charles said, sounding more worried than ever.

Briana closed her eyes tight, she steadied her voice as much as she could. "Yes, I'm fine."

"Why haven't you been answering the phone? I was just getting ready to put out an APB on you."

"Something came up," she said, trying to sound nonchalant.

"Do you want to talk about it?"

This man was more then she deserved. With her eyes still shut tight, she said, "Yes, I'm on my way home."

Charles let out an audible breath. He was happy about that. "Okay, I'll see you in a few."

"Okay," Briana responded.

"I love you," he said.

Her eyes opened meeting Justin's heartbroken stare. "I love you too," she responded.

They ended the call. She tossed the phone back in the car. How was she supposed to go home and face Charles? How was she supposed to tell him she was already married? Being married to Justin would nullify her and Charles' marriage that they'd consummated on more than one occasion. Briana could barely breathe as anger bubbled up in her gut. She was mad, and someone had to pay for this.

With the breath she could muster, through gritted teeth, she asked Justin, "Where is Tiana?"

# Chapter Seventeen

Tiana's phone was blowing up. It wouldn't stop ringing for sixty seconds before it started back up again. At first it was her mother, bothering her to no end. She never thought she would stop calling, but when she did it was her father. Seeing his number led Tiana to let out a string of profanity. The last person she wanted to deal with was her father. He would surely disown her after this. Next was Justin, he was calling more than her mom now. His number had been constant for the last two hours.

She paced the floor in Chris' kitchen, a wine glass in her hand that was now empty after her fourth refill.

"Baby, is everything okay?" Chris asked, stepping into the kitchen. He'd been watching her for the better part of an hour.

"Not really, I got into a fight with my sister and my mother." She let out a deep breath. "I don't know if our relationship will ever be the same."

"I'm sorry to hear that, your sister seems like a nice person."

Tiana peered at Chris. "You say that like you know her," she said.

"I met her and her husband… um, Justin, right? At the restaurant downtown."

Tiana had almost forgotten about that. She breathed a sigh of relief. She needed Chris in her corner, especially since it looked like he would be the only one there for a while. How could she let this happen? Everything was working out so well. Where did everything go wrong? Things fell apart, all in one day. Now that she thought about it, it was all her mother's fault. If she'd have kept her nose out of Tiana's business, none of this would be happening.

She thought about her niece, Denise Gable. It wasn't her fault she'd told her grandma the secret vow they'd made. She was a child after all, but she'd made it clear not to tell anyone. She huffed, kids couldn't be trusted. They couldn't hold water, so what made her think Denise would hold it for her? Realistically, she'd held it for a while. The little girl didn't realize her mother was different until Tiana started missing mother daughter times, and forgetting to pick her up from school. Denise was young, but she wasn't dumb. She knew something wasn't right.

Chris walked up to her, placed his hands on her shoulders and looked her in the eyes. "Everything will be alright, families fight all the time. You guys will be back to normal before you know it."

That pep talk may have worked if Tiana and Briana were really having a normal fight, but Tiana knew better, and really she didn't care. She wasn't looking to get back in her sister's good graces. As for her mother, well… she shrugged. But she didn't want to lose Justin. He was all the man she'd ever wanted. He'd belonged to her. Briana stole him from her and she wanted to keep him.

Tiana was brewing up a thunderstorm inside her mind. She wasn't one to give up easy. She'd convinced herself that Justin really loved her, and not Briana. After all, they'd been together for almost a year now. She would remind him of that. All the things she'd changed, he'd loved it, and she would make sure he continued to love it, if it was the last thing she did.

She poured more wine into her glass and took a big gulp then planted a kiss on Chris. "I'm tired," she said. "Take me to bed."

Chris gave her a knowing look.

"Yeah, that's what I meant," she said, answering his silent question.

Tiana powered her phone off and set her wine glass on the countertop. Without uttering a single word, Chris picked her up and carried her upstairs. Tiana closed the blinds and pulled back the black curtains, trying to make the room as dark as possible. She didn't want to come out of that room for a week. If it was up to her, she'd have it her way. She was sure she could let things die down while she hid out for a while. Chris wouldn't mind.

## *Two Hours Earlier...*

The house that Briana once called her saving grace now loomed in front of her like a shadow, threatening to kill her very hopes and dreams. She'd been sitting outside for fifteen minutes and couldn't will her legs to get out of the car and go inside. If someone had told her yesterday that today would be one of the worst days since she'd woken up from the coma, she wouldn't have believed it. Or better yet, she would've stayed in bed.

Before leaving the law firm, Justin had begged her not to go. He'd apologized relentlessly and swore to get to the bottom of their situation. He'd expressed regret about not being there for her during a difficult time in her life.

"I had no idea you were even in an accident. Please don't leave me, baby, please don't leave," he begged, stepping so close to her they could've turned into one person.

She hung her head low, ashamed of what had become of them. How does two people who love each other go months without knowing they're apart? Briana knew the answer to that. For the last few years of their marriage, she and Justin had become distant. Their heavy work flow didn't allow them time to tend to their marriage, leaving things stale between them.

He kissed her on her forehead in the same spot Charles had kissed her earlier. She looked up at him as tears continued to run down her cheeks, her eyes puffy and red. His scent was familiar, Curve for men, she'd picked it out for him and he still wore it to this day. It was a tiny thing that made a brief smile lift her lips.

Justin placed soft kisses on her eyes, on her tears, on her cheeks, her nose, her lips. More tears threatened to fall. She couldn't kiss him back without feeling like she was betraying Charles. She combed through her emotions, trying to figure it out. Who did she love more, or was that option even on the table? She was married to both men. She'd spent what felt like her whole life with Justin. The love she felt for him was for a lifetime.

Falling in love with Charles was like being in a fairytale. He'd been nothing but unconditionally good to her. He was the man of her dreams, a part of her life, the man she couldn't live without. So what was she going to do now? That was the question on her mind as she sat in front of her and Charles' home, staring at the front door.

She didn't get a chance to answer the question before the blinds moved. Briana took a deep breath and opened the car door. She had on her sunglasses that now covered her red rimmed puffy eyes. Charles met her at the door, his hands in the pockets of his Levi jeans. Even in the midst of all this pandemonium, Briana couldn't help but take in how tall he stood. His honey brown eyes boring a hole into hers, how his shirt fit his muscular frame, and his jeans fit his thighs, leaving just enough room for his wallet and keys. Oh, how handsome he was.

As she stepped in front of him, he reached out and pulled her inside, shutting the door behind them. There they stood in the entryway, holding each other. Briana buried her face in his chest, breathing in his scent. She wanted to stay there forever. All of a sudden, in the blink of an eye, life was unfair. She closed her eyes tight and took a deep breath.

"I remember," was all she said.

Charles pulled her back slightly and removed her sunglasses. He searched her eyes. "You've been crying." He wiped her tears. "What is it that you remember?" he asked.

Briana took another deep breath. "Everything."

Slowly, they pulled apart. Charles, shocked and interested by the sudden admission. "Would you like to sit down?" he asked.

Briana went over and plopped down on the sofa. Charles sat down next to her. He leaned over, resting his elbows on his thighs. Briana rested her back against the sofa, her head turned up toward the ceiling. As she stared, she said, "The little girl, her name is Denise Gable. She's my six-year old daughter."

Briana didn't know how much she should reveal to Charles at one time. Of course, he could handle it all, but should a person handle this much at one time? Lord knows she was a mess dealing with it. Her nerves were getting the better of her.

Charles showed no reaction. He was committed to hearing everything she needed to tell him before he did.

"I also have a teenage daughter. Her name is Taylor Gable. My name is Briana Gable, I'm…" she paused.

Tears sprang from her eyes and she collapsed, balling up into a fetal position. Her body rocked and she fell sideways into Charles' arms. He consoled her and tried to calm her down.

Hysterically, she cried and shouted, "Why would she do this to me?" By *she* Charles assumed she meant her sister. "Why! Why! Why! Why!"

Charles tightened his hold on her. "I'll never let her hurt you again," he said. "Not as long as I'm alive. You'll always be safe with me. I'll never let anyone hurt you again," he promised.

This made Briana cry even harder. She had a fleeting thought about staying with him and never telling him about Justin, but she could never do that. She had children, and how could she stay with him when she still loved Justin?

"I love you, I love you, I love you," he chanted.

She crawled into his lap, facing him. She stuck her tongue down his throat, their lips meshing together soft and hard, sweet and spicy. Her tears coating his cheeks, running down his face as if they were his own. At once, Briana pulled back. She never wanted to look away from him, never wanted to be away from him, never wanted to hurt him.

"She did it on purpose," Briana said. "I was in the car headed home from work. We were talking on the phone and she was going on and on about how I always got everything I wanted." As Briana told her story, she looked off into the distance, her eyes set in a faraway gaze. "She wants what I have, says I took it from her."

Confused, but not wanting to stop her, Charles listened patiently. "She cut the brakes on my car." More tears ran fast down her face. "At least I think she cut them, if she didn't, she got someone to do it. I didn't want to argue with her anymore. I asked her how I could help her and she said I was the one that needed the help. She asked me how fast I was going in my car, then told me good luck trying to stop." Briana's hands covered her weeping face. "She tried to kill me," she said, completely distressed.

Charles was boiling over on the inside. "We have to go to the police."

"I can't."

"Yes, you can!"

"No," she shook her head violently. "I can't," she repeated.

"Why not?"

"What am I supposed to tell them, that earlier this year my sister tried to kill me and I didn't know it all this time because I lost my memory, but now I remember after seeing my husband at work today?" She blurted it out before she had any chance of stopping it.

Charles paused and slowly rose to his feet. "What was that last thing you just said?" he asked.

Briana shut her eyes tight, balling her hands into a fist. Slowly, she opened her eyes and relaxed her palms. "I'm married," she said.

Still confused, Charles said, "You mean you're married to someone else?"

"His name is Justin Gable."

Silence. For ten agonizing minutes, no one spoke. Charles stood stone faced, his honey brown eyes weighing down on Briana like quicksand, threatening to pull her under. "Say something," Briana said.

"What do you want me to say?"

"Anything," she replied.

His hands slid down his face and he sucked his teeth. "You're married. You have been all this time?"

"Apparently," she said.

Charles started to laugh, it started out normal then turned disparaging. "So where has he been all this time? Where did he think his wife was, and why hasn't he been looking for you?" Before Briana could respond, Charles threw more questions at her. "Where has your family been? You were in the hospital for six months before you even came out of your coma, where have they been?" he screamed, anger boiling in his gut.

Briana got to her feet, her heart racing a mile a minute. "I don't know! He said he didn't even notice I was gone because Tiana pretended to be me. I know it sounds crazy, but she'd been—"

He interrupted her. "Sound crazy? NO that's just looney tunes! How does a man not know when his wife is not his wife? What kind of a man…" he trailed off. "So wait…" There was that pained laugh again. "He's been sleeping with her all this time, thinking she was you?"

Charles thought about Tiana. She clearly looked identical, but her attitude was completely different. He'd noticed that at the restaurant when he first met her. Briana was quiet. "So I guess that's it then, huh? I knew it. All this time, deep down, I always knew you were too good to be true. That this relationship was too good to be true."

"Don't say that. Our love is true!"

"Really?" he asked.

"How can you ask me that?" She got in his face. "I'm in love with you. I can't help what happened or how this turned out, but I'm in love with you, unequivocally, indisputably, undeniably, in love with you!" Her lips trembled. "Please, please, understand I didn't ask for any of this. I married you here and now, in this time because I love you, and I don't want to live without you."

"And what about him?"

"What about him?" she asked.

"Do you love him?"

"I love you," she said.

"Yeah, but do you love him?"

She didn't respond.

He shook his head up and down. "Right," he said.

"Listen, baby, please, I don't know what to do. I mean, what am I supposed to do? I have kids, a whole life over there, what am I supposed to do?"

"Do what you need to do," he said.

He walked around her and disappeared into the kitchen. She heard glass shatter and she cringed. Never ending tears flowed from her, so much so, that she was sure she'd drown in them. She ran to her bedroom and shut the door. It was as if he was blaming her for the way things had turned out. She knew it would hurt him, but she didn't take into consideration that he might blame her. Her heart throbbed like never before. She didn't want to leave, she wanted to stay, but how could she? Not with her daughters at home, she didn't have a choice.

She went to the closet and pulled out a suitcase. She trembled as she opened it and started to throw things in. As she moved around the room, her vision clouded and she wept. She heard more glass shattering and she slowed her movements. She leaned her body weight on the dresser and cried her eyes out. The vibrations in her sadness made her sick. Quickly, she grabbed the small garbage can that sat next to the dresser and gagged, her body threatening to regurgitate her breakfast. Nothing came out.

She slumped on the floor, weeping and praying to God. After a few minutes, she picked herself up and continued to gather her belongings.

The door to her bedroom opened. Charles walked in and

grabbed her. They fell against the wall as he pressed his body fiercely against hers. He crushed his mouth to hers and she melted in his arms. Their mouths did a mating dance, licking and kissing, sucking and devouring each other. He grabbed her bottom and lifted her, and her legs instantly wrapped around his waist. He put her against the wall, lifting her hands over her head. His mouth moved from her lips to her face, ears, and neck. He pulled at her t-shirt and tugged down her pants.

"You… belong… to… ME!" he panted.

Briana didn't object, she let him have his way with her.

"I would never mistake you for another woman! Not even your twin sister! You know why, because I know the rhythm of your heartbeat." He kissed and sucked against her skin like it was his last supper. "I could never mistake your love for someone else's. Never! Ever! Do you hear me?" he boomed. "I'm not letting you go! You don't get to run away from me after what we've been through together! He is your past. I am your future, and I will have what's mine," he growled. "Do you love me?"

"Yes," she whispered.

"I didn't hear you," he said.

"Yes! Yes! Yes! I love you forever with everything that I am," she panted.

"Tell me you belong to me," he said.

"I do, I do, I belong to you, Charles."

He crushed his mouth to hers and they didn't pull apart until they had made love on that wall, on the floor, the bed, they used everything for props, the dresser, the suitcase, and even the windowsill. When they'd thought they were completely spent, they came together again, never getting enough of each other.

## *Across Town...*

Terri opened the door to the three-bedroom home in Stone Mountain, Georgia. Her son in law looked like he'd had the wind slapped out of him. At the anguish on his face, she knew he'd already learned what she wanted to ask him about. She opened the door wider.

"Come in."

He walked past her through the foyer into the kitchen.

His father in law entered the kitchen with a bottle of Brandy in his hand. "Reach up in that cabinet above your head and pull those two glasses out," he said. Justin did as he was told. Gill turned to his wife. "Give us a moment of privacy, please." She kissed him on his cheek and left the room to tend to her granddaughters. "Sit down, son," Gill said.

"If you don't mind, I'd rather stand."

"Suit yourself."

Justin slid the glasses over to him. Gill retrieved a couple of ice cubes, put a few in each glass, then poured just a small amount of Brandy in each glass. He slid a glass over to Justin.

Instantly, Justin picked the small glass up and threw back the liquor. The glass clanked when he returned it to the table and slid it back to his father in law.

Gill eyed him then poured another small amount into his glass. The men stood there drinking for about fifteen minutes before either of them spoke.

It was Justin who spoke first. "I didn't know," he said.

Gill took a swig of his drink. "I hoped not. Now, I know my girls have pulled some stunts in their day. Especially in school. Whenever they got caught, Briana was always the one that took the blame. I understood then it was just child's play. What young adult wouldn't pull an ol' switcheroo when they have an identical twin? I'm sure all twins have done it at one time or another." He paused. "But this, I surely do not understand."

Justin stretched and popped his neck, turning his head from side to side.

"Are you telling me, that's what this was?" Gill asked.

Justin looked at him, astonished. "You think your daughters would do something like this on purpose?"

"Why don't you tell me what it is?" he said.

Justin gave him the details of his conversation with Briana. As he talked, he watched his father in law's facial expressions go from worry, surprise, and then disappointment.

"So this is where we are right now. Your daughter, Tiana, has been pretending to be Briana, and now she won't answer her phone."

Gill poured more Brandy into his glass and waved over Justin's glass. At this rate, they could go all night. "Where is Briana now?"

Justin leaned against the kitchen sink and folded his arms. "She went back to him."

Gill stared at Justin unblinking, letting everything he'd just been told register. "You didn't notice a single thing, son?" he asked.

"I noticed a lot of things. Her changing her job, and being more spontaneous. I noticed it all, but I didn't think it was because she was a completely different person. I thought she just wanted to keep the spice up in our marriage, I thought she just wanted a change of careers, people are allowed to do those things, right? Me, as her husband, I'm supposed to support her, not think 'oh, this must not be my wife'!"

Justin was more than frustrated. He couldn't bear to think that he'd lost the woman he'd spent his whole life with. Not one day went by when he didn't think about her, what he could do to make her life better, how he could surprise her.

The trip to Barbados for Pete's sake was for her, not Tiana. He shuddered at the thought. The things that he'd done with her sister. His mind went back to the day they had sex and she asked him to call her Tiana. Again, it was weird, and Justin had questioned her about it and told her to never ask him to do it again.

He shook his head; he couldn't be more repulsed by his actions. There was so much damage that had been done, and to know his own six-year-old daughter had noticed the change. But every time he questioned Tiana she had the perfect excuse, it made him all the more sick to his stomach. He thought about the boarding school conversations he and Tiana had. He had been completely lied to. The wool pulled over his eyes, all of the signs there, and he'd believed every word she said.

"Did you like it, son?" Gill asked.

Justin whipped his head up out of his reverie. He glared at his father in law. "Excuse me?"

"You heard what I said, did you like it?" Justin bit down on his teeth, his jaw clearly tight from the question. "Before you go all Rambo on me," Gill said. "I want you to take a second and think about it. You saw all the signs. I'm not asking you did you like Tiana. I'm asking you did you like the change?"

Justin rubbed his jaw and thought better about the question. He stretched his neck again. "I thought it was good for our marriage. To be honest, things had gotten a little stale between me and Briana, so sure I liked the changes. It wasn't a bad thing." Justin thought about what he'd just said, and sighed. "What are you getting at, Gill?"

"Maybe you didn't look harder into the changes because you didn't want to. Maybe you were happy with the way things were changing."

Justin slammed his glass down. "Listen, I'm human, sure

I like the fact that our relationship had gotten spicier, what man wouldn't? But in no way did I want it to be with another woman. I love Briana!"

"I'm sure you do, son. I'm not disclaiming that one bit, but you love Tiana too. You can't have them both."

"Are you serious? Do you hear yourself right now?" Justin said.

"You should ask yourself if you really want Briana back because getting her back would be going back to the way things were. She would more than likely be back at the law firm, she'd be at church with you every Sunday like clockwork. There probably won't be any whips or chains in the bedroom."

Justin gawked. "Whips or chains!"

"I'm just saying, son, whatever Tiana was doing that spiced your love life up, that will be gone, and the way things were would be back. Now I know you love Briana, and if she can find it in her heart to forgive you for sleeping with her sister..." Gill shook his head, still in disbelief that it had happened this way. "Then you should know for sure that's what you really want." Justin took the last sip of his Brandy and dropped the glass in the sink then went for the front door. He was steaming. He could hear his father in law's voice gaining on him. "Now, son, don't take what I'm saying the wrong way. For Briana's sake, think about it."

Justin rounded on him. "What you're really asking me to do is let her be happy with who she's with, if that's what she wants, right?" His teeth were showing. If he'd been an animal, Gill would've been all but eaten alive.

"Don't put words in my mouth, son. You both have some soul searching to do. Now I plan to talk to Briana and I'll tell her the same thing."

"Like hell you will!" he growled.

That little outburst took Gill be surprise. "And here I thought you were a Christian man," Gill said.

Justin ignored him. "You will not tell my wife she needs to do some soul searching. She belongs at home with me and her children. That's the end of the story." With that, he turned and went out the door. The engine to his Cadillac Escalade revved and he backed out of the driveway on his way home.

# *Chapter Eighteen*

## *One Week Later...*

Justin tossed aside a stack of legal papers that were for a new high profile case assigned to him. He'd thrown himself into work ever since finding out his wife was not his wife after all. He worked the midnight hour, some nights not making it home. Gill and Terri had his children, and although he missed them, he couldn't let them see him like this. His heart hurt so badly, and as a grown man, he'd never been broken down the way he was right then. He'd prayed to God on several occasions, wondering what he'd done to deserve this. Hadn't he given to the poor enough? Hadn't he loved his neighbor like he'd love himself? Why would this happen to him?

Justin already knew the answer to that question. Just because he was a man of God didn't mean bad things wouldn't happen to him. If anything, because he was a man of God, bad things were guaranteed to happen to him. Of course their marriage would be attacked, compromised, or destroyed. Briana hadn't called. He didn't have her number, and she hadn't picked up the phone and dialed him at all. He was sure of it because he'd waited on his cell phone to ring. He couldn't believe it. His wife, his love, his forever, and yet they were so disconnected it was unreal. Thoughts of his actions haunted him. There were red flags for sure and he had questioned them, but Tiana was good, really good. He couldn't get over the fact that he been so easily fooled.

He had stopped trying to contact Tiana. She'd turned her phone off and disappeared. The house was as quiet as a tomb. No life lived there. Over the days, Justin had thought of putting it up for sale. Why should he continue to live in it? He couldn't, wouldn't live in it. It had been tainted, disrupted, disrespected. He'd let Briana pick out their next home if she'd have him back. There was a knock at the door.

"What is it?" he said, not looking up.

"Mr. Gable, you have a visitor."

"I thought I told you to hold all my calls, and no visitors, Mary Lee. I'm too busy and I don't have time to talk to..." his voice trailed off once he looked up and saw her. He blinked several times, trying to make sure she wasn't a figment of his imagination.

"If you're busy," Briana said, "I can come back when you have some time."

Justin stood up slowly never taking his eyes off of her. "I have all the time in the world for you," he said. "Thanks, Mary Lee," he offered, dismissing her.

He rounded his large cherry wood office desk and pulled Briana in the room, closing the door behind her. Standing in front of her, he went over every detail of her face, still chastising himself for not knowing there was an intruder in their home.

"Do you mind if I sit down?"

"Of course not."

Briana sat down and crossed her legs. She wore a white

button down blouse with suspenders draped across her breasts, clamped to a pair of black skinny work pants. Her hair was pinned in a neat and clean ponytail that hung down, touching the nape of her neck. Once again, he noticed the absence of the tattoo and ground his teeth together. He sat with his hips on the edge of the desk in front of her, his sleeves rolled up to his elbows.

"You're beautiful," he said.

She blushed. "Thank you."

"I've waited for you to call," he said.

"I know. I've needed some time to take everything in, you know. Sorry for making you wait."

She relaxed in her chair. "I see you're hard at work as usual," she said.

"Oh, so you think you know me now?" he said jokingly.

She smirked. "Ha, ha, very funny."

"I miss you," he said. "I'm sorry. Please forgive me. I need you to forgive me."

Silence.

They watched each other. Briana closed her eyes briefly then opened them.

"Do you still love me?" Justin asked.

There it was. She knew it would come, but not so soon. She'd hoped to keep the conversation light for as long as possible, but it didn't take any time for it to turn serious.

"Justin…"

He got down on his knees, uncrossing her legs and placing his torso between them. She looked into his eyes.

"Please forgive me," he said.

"I do," she said. "I honestly didn't know if I could, but I do. As for my sister, I will never trust her again. And I'll never trust you around her."

"You won't have to worry about me being around her. I don't want to be," Justin promised. "Will you come home?"

There was more silence.

"Things can't just go back to the way they were. So much has changed," Briana said.

"We can make things better, we can get back to the way we were."

"I'm not so sure," Briana said.

"The night before our wedding, we promised never to let anything tear us apart, no matter how bad things got. Do you remember that?"

Briana shut her eyes briefly. "Yes, I do."

"Does that still hold true?"

When she didn't respond, his head fell into her lap. He put his arms around her waist, snuggling her. She could feel the warmth from his breath on her thighs. She almost jumped out of her skin. She had to get away from him. She did remember making that promise. It was the vow before the vows. Being near him reminded her of their life, of their love, of their promises. She put her arms around him.

"Let's start over," he said. "We deserve to give it another chance, especially for the kids' sake."

He was right, she had all but come to the office today to declare her love for Charles and to let him know they could work out arrangements with the children. But who was she kidding? Could she really split her kids up like that? She couldn't think about herself more than she thought of them.

"I don't know, I just… it would take some time for me to adjust. I can't stay in that house," she revealed.

"I didn't think you would want to. I'm putting it up for sale."

"We should have a conversation with Tiana."

"Why?" he asked.

"Don't you want to get down to the bottom of this?"

"I don't want to talk to her ever again," he said. "Not in this life or the next. She has singlehandedly destroyed our marriage."

"We still need to talk to her. I do, I want to know why she needed to go to these extremes."

"I'll support whatever decision you make," he said.

"I want you to contact her, she won't respond to me," Briana stated.

"I've been trying to contact her and she's not responding to me either."

"Send her a text message, let her know you're not mad, and just want to talk. Wherever she's hiding, she'll come out."

"What makes you so sure?" he asked.

"Because in her mind, you belong to her."

*Briana is right,* Justin thought. He wanted to know why Tiana felt this way. He pulled out his cell phone and sent her a text.

*We need to meet. I just want to talk to you. No hard feelings, Tiana. Meet me at the house today. Let me know if you will.*

He sent the message and waited for a response.

"Have you had lunch?" Briana asked.

"I can't remember the last time I ate," he responded.

She lifted his head from her lap and checked out his face. "I'm going to order some Chinese food from China Dragon, do you want your usual?"

He smiled. "Yes."

His phone dinged, it was an incoming text message. *Meet me at seven tonight.* Justin showed Briana the text message. She inhaled then exhaled, knowing this meeting could get out of hand.

"It's amazing how quickly she responded, and I've been trying to get in touch with her all week."

"That's because she thought she was in trouble. Now she thinks you just want to have a civilized conversation with her. Something is definitely wrong in her head."

Briana made the phone call and ordered the Chinese food. As she ordered, she thought about Charles. Realistically, she needed a lawyer to sort these things out. The problem was she didn't want to divorce Charles, she didn't think she really could, but she could go to jail being married to two men at the same time. Life had gone from being full of bliss to more frustrating than the day she woke up in the hospital not knowing her name.

Justin rose from his place on the floor and proceeded to clear his desk, so when their lunch arrived they could eat. He dared not ask Briana if she was in love with what's his name. He didn't care, it wouldn't make a difference one way or the other because she belonged to him.

After leaving his in laws house earlier in the week, he'd given some thought to what Gill had said. He did like the change, but not at the expense of never being with Briana again. She was all he'd ever wanted, and he'd told Tiana on more than one occasion that he liked things the way they were. The more he'd thought about Tiana's deception, the angrier he became.

When the food arrived, they ate in silence. Every once in a while, they'd look up at each other, giving tiny smiles and wondering what the other was thinking.

"What are you thinking?" Justin said.

Briana waited until he'd taken his last bite before she admitted it. She wanted him to eat, and who knew when would be the next time he ate after her admission. "I love him," she said.

Justin put his fork down. The last bit of food he'd just taken sat in his throat, unable to go down. Briana watched his mood change, but she didn't regret what she'd said.

"He's taken care of me ever since the accident. He's been nothing but a gentleman." Justin finally swallowed but didn't respond. "He's waiting for me to come back." Briana watched every inch of him, giving him only a little at a time. "I'm pregnant," she said.

Justin sat back. The very air he breathed was sucked out of the room. Every part of him felt like a stab of pain that ricocheted through his very being.

"No," he whispered. "You want to have his baby?" Justin asked.

Briana's eyebrows lifted. "I didn't think it would happen so soon, but yes," she said.

It was a hard pill for Justin to swallow. "You can't have his baby," he said, shaking his head no. "What would we tell the kids? They already know you're not the person that's been in the house. How would they react to you having a baby?" He continued to shake his head no. "It can't happen. You've got to get an abortion."

Briana gasped. "Have you lost your mind?"

"How could I not?" he said. "You're my wife, and you're having another man's baby."

Tears glazed Briana's eyes. "I'm his wife also, and you don't get to tell me what I can and can't do! You don't love me," she said softly.

"What?" Justin said. "That's what it boils down to? Because I'm not willing to let my wife have another man's baby, I don't love you?"

"I'm his wife too!"

Justin guffawed. "We both know our marriage is the one that counts." He sighed. "Let me ask you something, if Tiana had been pregnant with my baby, would you have been okay with it?"

"Of course not!" Briana said. "But I wouldn't have asked you for an abortion!"

Justin put his hands up in surrender. "You're right. I'm sorry, that was a horrible thing to ask for," he said. "Adoption, or you can just give your parental rights over to him, and he can be on his way."

Briana shook her head. "I could never do that, and I haven't said I was leaving him."

"Well what are you going to do?" he asked, getting impatient.

"Listen, I know all of this is hard, and because this is new and alarming, I'll forgive the fact that you've asked me twice to give up a baby that's growing inside of me. I know you were blindsided by it, and I know we are against abortions. So we should pick this conversation up later."

Justin agreed. He looked down at his watch. It was six o'clock. "We better get going if we want to meet Tiana."

They got up and made their way to the door. Justin reached out and grabbed Briana's hands before they exited. She turned her face to him and he placed a small simple kiss on the side of her forehead before they left.

Tiana pulled in front of the mailbox of the house she once called home. She took a look around to see if there was anybody following her. Being in hiding had made her paranoid, to say the least. She couldn't turn her phone on without getting a barrage of phone calls or messages. She'd thought being in hiding would calm things down a bit. But instead, it seemed to make more of a hail storm.

Chris, however, was enjoying her stay at his home. Every day he would mention how good it would be to come home to her in the evenings. Tiana had nothing against Chris, he was a good man, but she wanted what she wanted, and that was Justin. She exited the car and went to the front door, using her key to let herself in. The house was quiet. Of course the children wouldn't be there.

Tiana was there with high hopes. She hoped things would go in her favor and she would no longer have to worry about pretending to be someone else. She could just be herself. She wore a red button down cat like body suit that fit every angle to perfection. The pants on the jumpsuit stopped mid-calf, exposing the red Monolo Blahniks. Her shoes click clacked on the floor as she entered the living space.

"I'm in the kitchen," came the voice she'd missed since leaving their humble abode.

She bit her bottom lip and smiled. Her footsteps made quicker strides to get to him. She rounded the corner and stepped into the kitchen. When his eyes fell on her, she melted on the inside. He was babysitting a small glass of rum on the rocks. Next to him sat a wine glass filled half way, that hadn't been touched. Smiling, she went to him. She picked up the wine glass and took a sip. Never taking her eyes off of him.

"Sure, you can have my wine," Briana said, cutting the corner and stepping into the kitchen. "It seems you've gotten used to taking what's mine lately."

Tiana cut her eyes at Briana's entrance. She set her wine glass down, a sour taste now invading her mouth. "Really," she said. Tiana looked at Justin and clapped her hands softly. "You set me up, how very sneaky of you." Her voice was soft, low and calculated.

"How did you find out, dear sister? Was it my loving husband, or did you finally get your memory back? She set her red and black clutch down and lifted herself onto the countertop, crossing her legs, making sure to give Justin a close up of what he'd been missing. Her eyes taunted Briana and her tongue teased the top of her red cherry lips.

"You're sick, Tiana, you need to get some help. Justin is my husband, not yours. He's always belonged to me, never you. And for the record, yes, I got my full memory back, no thanks to you."

"I always knew you'd get your memory back." Tiana sighed. "So, I guess this Is where you bombard me with questions of why, and accusations of how could you and blah blah blah," she said.

Justin and Briana glanced at each other and back to Tiana. "Actually," he said. "I, for one, would like to know why."

"Ah," Tiana said, holding up a manicured finger. Her leg bounced softly. "You really don't get it, do you?" She sighed. "Do you remember the first time we met, Justin? We were at a baseball game. You were standing in line at the concession stand. It was then that we had our moment, it was a fleeting moment, but I know we felt a pull toward one another. I was looking for her," she said, glancing Briana's way. "After going in the bathroom to find her, I got the guts to approach you, only to find her with you once I exited. She could never stand to let me have what I so rightfully deserved. Nooo, instead, she had to have it for herself."

"You remember that, but you couldn't remember the case I just recently won?" he said sarcastically.

Tiana gave him a sideways glance. "You still don't forgive me for that, do you? Well, counselor, in my defense, I did have a lot going on. You know, trying to be your wife and all." Her smirk was eerie and wicked. "Like I was saying before, I had my eye on you, then your head slightly turned my way and our eyes met. As a matter of fact, you winked and I blew you a kiss. I excused myself and went to the bathroom to freshen up, and when I got back, you were talking to her." Her eyes cut daggers at Briana. "I watched her butter you up and stick you in the oven so she could have you for dinner." Tiana was still cutting daggers at Briana. "But did she care?" She shook her head with a conniving smile on her face. "No, she didn't, she moved right in for the kill, and you took the bait. It's been the story of my life. So tell me, why should I care about her feelings now?"

There was silence in the room, everyone eyeing one another. Then Briana spoke up. "How was I supposed to know you had your eye on him? You never mentioned it! If you'd have pointed him out, maybe you would have him. But you didn't, did you?

"That is beside the point," Tiana said.

"You can't be serious. We've been in a relationship, had children, gotten married, and you're still holding that grudge." Briana shook her head. "You're sick. My husband doesn't want you, get over it. And I want to know what really happened to Angela."

"Mmmm, maybe he does," Tiana said, ignoring Briana's last statement. "So, sweetheart," she said, looking at Justin. "Do you still want me or do you want to go back to your boring housewife?"

Justin set his glass down. "Tiana, I want to apologize to you. I never thought that minute we shared would stir up all this. I want to also apologize for whatever I did to make you think I loved you, or was in love with you. It was not my intention to mislead you. I don't know how I was able to live with you for so long without realizing you weren't my wife. After speaking to Gill the other day, he asked me to make sure it was Briana I wanted and not you. I guess he felt because I'd spent so much time with you, putting off all of the changes that you supposedly made being Briana, that somehow deep down inside I really wanted you. The fact is, I welcomed the change because it was refreshing. Our relationship had become stagnant, but all relationships can use spontaneity at times. So it's not that I didn't want to notice you were not my wife. It's that I genuinely thought she'd just spiced up our life." He turned to Briana. "I don't know how, but if you could ever find it in your heart to forgive me, I would make it my life's mission to make this right."

Tiana slid off the countertop and stepped in front of Justin, cutting his view off from Briana. "You don't need her. She'll never be able to give you spontaneity. That's all me! She will never be the wife you need. Don't you get that?" She grabbed his hands." I love you, there is no need for you to apologize for being happy with what I gave you. You can keep it. I'll give you more, and then some. You'll forget all about her. You don't need her!"

Justin felt sorry for Tiana, he really did. She just didn't understand she would never be the one he chose. It would always be Briana. He pulled back from her, "Tiana, you should leave. We've got a lot of rebuilding to do, and it would be better if you didn't come around."

Her eyes glistened, her heart filled with pain. Justin stepped around her and went to Briana. He grabbed her hands.

"I already told you I forgive you," she said. "Don't ask me to say it again."

He kissed her on her forehead and she closed her eyes.

Tiana's hands shook, her face turning medieval. She grabbed her clutch and pulled out the three eighty handgun she'd retrieved from her glove compartment just before entering the house. Without saying one word, she turned to Briana and aimed.

Justin cut his eyes at her in time to see her pull the trigger.

"NO!" he screamed, shielding Briana with his five foot eleven-inch frame.

The bullet ripped through his chest, sending him and Briana crashing to the floor.

"JUSTIN!" Both twins screamed at the same time.

Tiana ran to him as Briana crouched down on the floor next to him. She looked up at Tiana and back at Justin, tears streaming down her face.

"No, no, no, no, baby please," she begged.

Justin touched the side of Briana's face. His breathing labored and light. She ran for her phone but Tiana tackled her to the floor. They wrestled and rolled over each other, one slapping the other. Huffing and puffing, pants and shouts coming from each of the girls.

Tiana grabbed a handful of Briana's hair and banged her head against the floor. Saliva flew from her mouth. "This is all your fault. You want to know what happened to Angela, huh? I killed her! She was too nosey and getting in my way, so she had to be disposed of!" she screamed. Briana was starting to feel lightheaded and she knew she would soon pass out.

Tiana clawed at her face. She punched then stood and kicked her in her back and abdomen over and over. It was over for Briana; this would be her end. A gun shot rang out in the distance. Briana knew she was dead. She lay in a heap on the floor, her body shaken to its core. There was a loud thud. She opened her eyes to see Tiana fall to her knees and lay in a pool of her own blood, right next to her.

Justin, on his knees, dropped the gun and fell to the floor, a warm red flowing from his chest. Sirens blared, getting closer as someone in the neighborhood had surely called the police after hearing the first gun shot. Briana crawled over to him.

"Justin!" When she got to him, she could see his life fading, "No, Justin, please!" she screamed. Lying next to him holding him tight, she rocked, "Help is on the way. Hold on." That was the last thing Justin heard, before a soft blanket of darkness covered him.

The house stood still and unmoving. When the paramedics arrived, they called for backup. They would need more stretchers than they had realized.

"Ma'am can you tell us what happened?" The first responder asked.

"He doesn't have a pulse," someone else said.

From the dining room, another man said, "She doesn't have a pulse either!"

The emergency response crew worked on both Justin and Tiana. An EMS assessed Briana's injuries and decided she needed further medical attention. They strapped her to a gurney. Briana was in a daze as everything around her moved in slow motion. She couldn't comprehend anything, and soon she was on her way to the hospital.

# Epilogue

## *One Year Later*

"Yes ma'am, cut the stem off please." Charles paid the cashier for two bouquets of white and yellow calla lilies and a bouquet of red and pink roses. It was the one-year anniversary of that horrible day back in August. A day he would never forget.

He'd gotten an emergency call from the hospital, and like usual, he rushed to be by Briana's side. She'd been beaten so badly her eyes were a purplish color and swelling by the minute. She'd had cracked ribs and had been in a slumber for hours. It was only after the surgeons finished working on her that they were able to contact him. Being on Briana's next of kin list had been a nightmare so far. He'd gotten more calls about her being in the hospital than anything.

He pulled up to Oakland Cemetery and found the burial plots he was looking for. He parked alongside the gravel and exited his truck. The sun shone bright in the sky onto the freshly maintained green grass of the cemetery. His steps sped up as he saw her standing in front of the headstones, sunglasses covering her face. She wore a black blouse with sleeves that stopped just above the elbows, blue jeans, and two inch heels. Her hair whipped as the wind rode waves through her straight mane.

He approached her in silence, handing her a bouquet of calla lilies. A small smile touched her face as she received them. On her toes, she crouched down in a squatting position and removed built up dirt and weeds that had grown over the headstone. The front of it read,

**Tiana Williams**
**July 22, 1978 – August 7, 2014**
**Gone, but not forgotten**

Briana placed the Calla lilies on her grave and said a small prayer. It was surreal that her twin lay buried in this grave. Briana went over it in her head so many times, wondering what if. As much as Tiana had hated her, she still loved her with all her heart. She could never have such hatred in her heart as Tiana did. Briana wondered if she could've gotten her help would she still be alive today and thriving, but she would never know. Her sister was gone too soon, and she would forever weep and miss her. Briana moved to the grave next to Tiana's, it read,

**Justin Gable**
**September 8, 1977 – August 8, 2014**
**A loved father and husband**

"Are you ready for them?" Charles asked.

Briana shook her head up and down. This was the hardest part of this visit. Seeing her husband's headstone always shattered her to pieces. She would never forget waking up in the hospital and seeing the sorrowful look in Charles eyes.

"Where's Justin? Where's Tiana?" she asked.

Charles had hesitated to answer.

Tears had streamed down her face. "Where are they!" she screamed horrified at the reality.

"They didn't make it," he said.

A scream left her gut and pierced the air. Charles had held on to her as she wept. Briana had shed tears for Justin, for Tiana, for her kids that would never see their dad and aunt again. Briana cried until there were no more tears left. That was a year ago, and the pain still soaked her every time she made an appearance at their graves.

She waited until Charles walked away to get the girls before she broke down. She crouched in front of his headstone and removed the dirt and weeds that had grown on his headstone as well. She wept like it happened yesterday. A rush of memories ran through her mind. All of the things they'd been through together and all of the love they made. He'd left two children behind, and they were heartbroken to find out their father had died.

Taylor had blamed her mom for so long, Briana had gotten used to it. After getting Taylor counseling, she'd come to realize there was nothing her mom could've done differently, and that her dad had died saving her mom's life.

Taylor didn't want to visit Tiana's grave, and she was upset that it sat so close to her father's. A part of Briana blamed herself. She'd been out of her kid's life for too long and wasn't there to protect them. Deep down inside, she knew there was nothing she could've done differently. That didn't stop her from blaming herself, though.

At the funeral, Tiana's boyfriend, Christopher Summers, had showed up and broke down. It was clear he was in love with her. That left Briana with even more questions, and after having a heart to heart with him, she'd learned that he and

Tiana were pretty serious and talking about moving in together. That puzzled Briana, especially with the fiasco Tiana had created over Justin. That just showed Briana how many secrets Tiana kept and that she had misled a whole line of people.

After Tiana's admission about Angela, she thought it better of her if she sent her family her proper condolences. Enclosed in an envelope was a money order for five hundred thousand dollars. It was the least she could do, knowing that Angela took care of her parents. It would be enough money to pay off their house and cars and have a little extra left to put in their savings. She missed her friend like crazy.

Briana was Justin's beneficiary. She'd inherited his full fortune after his passing, and his life insurance policy, which was over two million dollars. She had more than enough money to take care of her kids.

The law firm had actually tried to get her to come back to work. With Justin gone, a group of their clients went in search of other law firms. Once Adler and Adams tried to get them to stay, assuring their cases would have success, they would only come back under one condition, and that was if they could get Mrs. Gable assigned to their case. Briana had no intention of going back to the firm, especially since it would remind of her Justin. But to pay tribute to him, she finished off his work load and won all of his cases.

Her life as a lawyer wasn't over. Briana had moved on and opened her own law firm, hiring some of Atlanta's most prestigious attorneys. Their case load was heavy, but in just a short time, they had a ninety percent success rate. She'd legally changed her name from Briana to Gabrielle Finnegan. Her relationship with Charles was all the more strengthened by the past years' events. They would surely be together forever. He was a wonderful stepfather, and the girls truly loved him.

Taylor and Denise crouched down next to their mom. They took Calla Lilies and placed them on their dad's grave. "Is he in heaven now looking down on us?" Denise asked. Briana turned her head toward her. "Of course he is," she said.

Briana pulled the girls in, hugging them as tight as possible. Charles stood back, giving his new family some room. He'd never thought he would ever have another family, but God saw fit to give him just that, and he was grateful every day for them. His daughter, Camilla Anne Finnegan, was born seven months after Briana's last hospitalization. The mere fact that she'd survived after the beating Briana had endured was a sign that God had indeed given them his blessing.

He held her in his arms, placing soft kisses on her smooth round cheeks and watched his family pay respect to their family. He would protect them and guide them, and make sure they were taken care of in all areas of their lives.

They now attended his church home, Mount Zion Missionary Baptist, and they'd become family there. Things were looking bright, and Charles was on the road to becoming the chief at the firehouse, pending Chief Richardson's retirement. Things couldn't be better, the only darkness in their life was this day every year, when he would have to watch his family mourn over the death of their loved ones.

He would take them out to eat, and enjoy a movie and ice cream later to get the girls' mind off of the gloomy day, and all would be well in the Finnegan household.

THE END

# About the Author

Stephanie Nicole Norris is an author from Chattanooga Tennessee with a humble beginning. She, along with her six siblings, were raised by her mother, Jessica Ward. Growing up a lover of reading, Stephanie loved to read books by R.L. Stine. She always had a natural talent for writing, and 2010 was the beginning of her journey. In early 2012, her debut novel, "Trouble in Paradise", was published. It is a dramatic romance about a 28-year-old African-American female, Victoria Mathis, who tries to better herself with an internship and marrying the love of her life. In doing so, she runs into roadblocks and things spiral out of control, causing major changes for her future.

Seven months later, Stephanie released her sophomore title, "Vengeful Intentions", which is part two of "Trouble in Paradise". September 27, 2014 Stephanie released "For Better and Worse", part 3 of "Trouble in Paradise". Coming May 2016 Stephanie's final installment to the Trouble in Paradise series titled "Until My Last Breath" will be released. Also, she has a series of short stories called The Lunch Break series. These stories are not continuations of the same story and can be read in your lunch break hour. The Lunch Break series, which features titles like "Wreckless" and "Broken", was inspired by the reader who doesn't have time to read a full novel and can be found on Amazon, Kobo and Barnes and Noble. Stephanie's words tell stories of love, drama, deception, suspense, and restoration. She is inspired by the likes of Victoria Christopher Murray, Vanessa Davis Griggs, Eric Jerome Dickey, Jackie Collins, Gwynne Forster, and more. She resides in between Atlanta, Georgia and Chattanooga, Tennessee.

Stephanie features authors of the Christian and/or Romance genre. (No erotica) If you're an author and would like to be featured on her blog, email her today at stephaniennorris@gmail.com

## Also by Stephanie Nicole Norris

Victoria is thankful for a lot of things- Joshua, the love of her life, a career change that starts a new chapter, and a condo in the suburbs of Chicago Illinois. Her jaw drops when she opens the garage and finds a brand new Cadillac wrapped in a huge bow. She is ecstatic and ready for the next steps towards her future. This is Victoria's fresh beginning.

When Victoria and Joshua start their journey things take a turn for the worse. Victoria finds out her nemesis and Joshua's ex, Danielle Shumaker has flown to Chicago to try to get Joshua back. Victoria is determined to win this fight, when she finds out Joshua has secrets of his own. Distraught, confused, and feeling the sting of betrayal she falls into the arms of another. When emotions run high and desire digs deep Victoria finds herself caught up in Trouble.

After serving eight long months in jail and becoming obsessed with the woman who put her there Danielle Shumaker is released when the evidence held against her comes up missing. With Victoria clouding her mind with thoughts of revenge Danielle is caught off guard when someone wants to make her pay for past transgressions.

Not needing the added drama Victoria is still torn between her feelings toward Greg and her undying love for Joshua. With new knowledge that Danielle has been released from jail; Victoria is stunned knowing Joshua has not been honest with her.

Things get hotter when Joshua catches wind of Victoria's affair and Caroline wants her husband back by any means necessary. Will this love story end in tragedy or will these couples learn to forgive and forget? Find out in part II of Trouble In Paradise.

Coming out of hibernation, Danielle Shumaker has put behind her the pain and misery she's caused Victoria and Joshua. Blinded by her selfishness her ultimate goal is still her main one. As far as Danielle's concerned Joshua belongs to her, always has and always will. No amount of therapy can cure her love addiction and no matter what anyone says she will fight for him, even if she has to kill someone AGAIN.

Wedding bells are in Victoria and Joshua's future, Victoria is excited to be Mrs. Eubanks. However, when she closes her eyes at night, Greg invades her dreams, the passion and love leaves her wanting more and waking with doubt about her upcoming marriage. How will she get over this man or does she even want to?

Jasmine Johnson wants nothing more than to be swept off her feet by classmate and cutie Maurice Desmon Jones. Everything about him, from his obvious confidence to his charisma, makes her melt like ice cream on a sundae cone.

One day, someone threatens to challenge her for his affection and Jasmine goes into a jealous rage, unable to control her emotions. Obsession sends her over the edge and there is no turning back. In the eye of a brewing storm, she has to come up with a clever way to get out of the catastrophe she has created and she won't give up, even if she has to die trying.

Relationships always start out rosy in the beginning, but they never last that way. At least this is what Marissa thought as she watched Nathaniel preparing to go out to God knows where at 11 o'clock at night. What used to be love had turned into regret — to the point that Marissa often despised being around him. Sure, they've had their break-ups and their make-ups. But this relationship had grown stale, boring, and sometimes depressing, and Marissa wanted out.

Now Joe, on the other hand, was handsome, flirtatious, and older. He had Christian values and knew what he wanted out of life. Marissa couldn't deny his obvious charm and magnetic pull towards her and she wanted to find out what being with him was like. However, being a Christian woman herself, her morals wouldn't allow her to cheat on Nathaniel, even if their relationship was practically over. Or maybe she could get a taste just once. Nathaniel didn't have to know, and God would forgive her, right? The struggle between knowing when a relationship has run its course or when it's time to stand strong is real. Is the grass really greener on the other side?

# Coming Soon!

LOVE IS A DRUG INK PRESENTS
UNTIL MY
LAST
BREATH
PART 4 OF TROUBLE IN PARADISE
STEPHANIE NICOLE NORRIS

Made in the USA
San Bernardino, CA
04 April 2016